THE Real Rebecca

Anna Carey

THE O'BRIEN PRESS
DUBLIN

First published 2011 by The O'Brien Press Ltd,
12 Terenure Road East, Rathgar, Dublin 6, Ireland.
Tel: +353 1 4923333; Fax: +353 1 4922777
E-mail: books@obrien.ie
Website: www.obrien.ie
Reprinted 2011 (twice)

ISBN: 978-1-84717-132-0

A catalogue record for this title is available from the British Library.

3 4 5 6 7 8 9 10
11 12 13 14 15

Layout and design: The O'Brien Press Ltd
Cover illustrations: Chris Judge
Printed and bound by CPI Group (UK) Ltd, Croydon, CR0 4YY
The paper in this book is produced using pulp from managed forests.

The O'Brien Press receives assistance from

Winner Specsavers Children's Book of the Year – Senior

'I laughed and squirmed my way through *The Real Rebecca*, the sparkling and spookily accurate diary of a Dublin teenager. It's stonkingly good and I haven't laughed so much since reading Louise Rennison. ' *Sarah Webb, author of the 'Amy Green' series*

'A really good teen book ...'
Sarra Manning, author of 'Diary of a Crush' and 'Fashionistas'

'This book is fantastic! Rebecca is sweet, funny and down-to-earth, and I adored her friends, her quirky parents, her changeable but ultimately loving older sister and the swoonworthy paperboy.' *Chicklish Blog*

'A laugh-out loud story.' *Hot Press*

'The dialogue crackles with authenticity and wry humour ...'
Irish Independent

'A funny light-hearted romp ...' *Irish Times*

'Brilliantly funny.' *Evening Herald*

'Rebecca is a thoroughly likeable heroine – angsty and mixed-up but warm-hearted and feisty.' *Books Ireland*

Anna Carey is a freelance journalist from Drumcondra in Dublin who has written for the *Irish Times*, *Irish Independent* and many other publications. Anna joined her first band when she was fifteen and went on to sing and play with several bands over the next fifteen years. Her last band, El Diablo, released two albums and toured all over the country. This is her first book.

ACKNOWLEDGEMENTS

Thanks to Susan Houlden, Emma Byrne and everyone at the O'Brien Press; Chris Judge for such a perfect cover; Helen Carr for support, friendship and inspiration; Jennifer Foster, Louise Butler and Miriam McCaul, who sat through many real-life history and German classes with me in Dominican College and are still my friends twenty years later; Sinéad Gleeson and everyone at the Anti-Room; Joan, Wally and all the Freynes, especially Maria for telling me about the Junior Cert history curriculum; my parents, who always encouraged their daughters' slightly deranged literary endeavours; my sisters Lisa, Jenny and Rachel for thirty-five years of shrieking and laughing; my nephew Arlo McGurk, aka Mr Baby, for being a general inspiration; and last but not least, to my husband Patrick Freyne for being brilliant and kind and making me laugh a lot.

To my parents, who are not quite as
embarrassing as the parents in this book,
and to my husband Patrick,
who is (almost) never embarrassing at all.

MONDAY ♥

Today is the first day of the new school year, and it's been raining non-stop since I woke up. Which is just typical, as Cass said this morning on the way to school. She had to keep taking her glasses off as we walked, because it was raining and she couldn't see through them. She says that being basically blinded by rain is just one more reason why she absolutely has to get contact lenses for her birthday, even though her parents think she should wait another year.

'But when you think about it,' said Alice, as Cass wiped her glasses on her school jumper for the fiftieth time, 'it's a good thing that it's raining today. Because if it was sunny, it'd be even worse having to go to school. You've got to count your blessings, Cass.'

And then she stood in a puddle that was more like a lake, and after that she stopped saying how great the rain was.

So here I am, Rebecca Rafferty, now the wonderful age

of fourteen and back in horrible St Dominic's again, writing in my diary in the middle of geography. Miss Kelly won't care because she's wittering on about the hideous effects of global warming, her favourite subject. All our classes were about it last year. It's quite handy, really – Miss Kelly always gets so excited by the thought of our impending hideous deaths that she doesn't care what we're doing in class as long as we're quiet. Alice and I have been having a conversation in note form, but now Alice's pen has run out so I'm writing this. Miss Kelly is in full flow now, so she'll never notice. I don't know why she's still telling us about melting ice caps and the forthcoming ice age; she terrified us into submission months ago. We have all vowed never to own cars. Lisa O'Hara even refused to go in her parents' car for a while, but she gave up when they said they'd drive off on holiday to France without her.

Anyway! School hasn't changed in the three months since I last saw it. It's the same hideous old kip it was last year. Everyone in our class is the same, although Jessie McCabe has dyed her hair blonde (she says her parents went mad when they saw it, not least because she paid for it with the money she'd been given to get new school shoes) and Vanessa Finn is possibly even more annoying than she was last year. Vanessa's parents are very rich and apparently her dad really wanted her to go to a private school because he didn't want her to attend the same school as, and I actually quote, 'girls who would grow up to be hairdressers'. Because according to him that is a fate worse than death. But of course there are no private schools anywhere near here so she would have had to go to town to find one, and giving her a lift there would take too long what with the deadly-fume-exuding traffic, so she's stuck at St Dominic's with the rest of us commoners.

So anyway, school is more or less the same as ever. In fact, the only difference is that we are no longer the youngest girls in the school. Hurrah! Cass and Alice agree with me that the first years all look about five. We can't have looked like that last year, can we? This lot don't look old enough to be allowed walk to school on their own.

I wonder if they've heard the rumours that first years get their heads flushed down the loos by evil sixth-year bullies. Alice and I were obsessed with those stories before we started at St Dominic's, even though Rachel told us they were rubbish. We thought she was just lulling us into a false sense of security, because that's what mean big sisters do, but it turned out she was actually right. Sixth years didn't flush first years down the loos. Although we wouldn't accept this until Christmas. We never went to the loo on our own in case a sixth year pounced on us from behind a cubicle door and shoved our heads down the toilet.

Oops, Miss Kelly seems to be winding down. She's got to what we'll do if we survive the ice age, which means that the class is nearly at an end. Better go.

LATER

I'm writing this at home, far away from the hell of St Dominic's School for Girls. Not that it's much better around here. I was just on the phone to Cass and my mother came into my room and STOOD OVER ME UNTIL I GOT OFF THE PHONE! What sort of mother is she? She doesn't want me to be able to talk to anyone. She and Dad only give me a tiny amount of credit for my phone so I have to use the landline if I want to have a proper conversation. And of course that means she hovers over me, telling me to hang up after about five minutes.

This evening she said that I'd been on the phone for over an hour and it was costing her and Dad money and when I was paying my own bills I could stay on the phone for as long as I liked but until then blah, blah, blah.

I said, in a very dignified voice, 'Mother, Cassandra and I have important scholastic matters to discuss. Please go away.'

She said, 'Oh, come off it, Bex, you were talking about that ridiculous programme about rich kids in Los Angeles, I could hear you from the kitchen.'

I said, 'American television drama is an important scholastic matter, mother dear. We're doing media studies this term.'

And she just laughed at me and said, 'Well, I'm sure your teacher will be very interested in hearing your thoughts on – what was it? The "incredible cuteness of Jack Rosenberg".'

I glared at her and said, 'The only attractive boys we ever see are on the telly, seeing as we're stuck in an all-girl school. Please don't deny us our only pleasure. Jack Rosenberg is the only romantic outlet we have.'

And she laughed again and said, 'One more minute,

Bex. I'm warning you.' She went off to the kitchen to laugh about me some more with Dad, but I knew she'd be listening to make sure I didn't stay on the phone for longer than sixty seconds. So I had to get off the phone. If all the women who read her stupid books knew what a terrible mother she was, they'd never buy another one of them again. Mum's books are all full of feisty old mothers who are the heart of their happy homes. They never force their innocent daughters to get off the phone when they are in the middle of discussing whether Jack Rosenberg is still as cute as he was in the first series of Laurel Canyon. (I say he's not; Cass says he only gets better with age).

Someday I will write an exposé on what my mother is really like. I said this to Rachel once and she just sniggered and said, 'Oh yeah, what'll you say? That she didn't let you rack up another 300 Euro phone bill? Boo hoo, you're so deprived.'

'She's your mother too, Rache,' I said. 'You should write one as well.'

And then Rachel got all serious and stern and told me to count my blessings because our parents are great (which is not what she thought a few months ago when they wouldn't let her go to Glastonbury with her boyfriend) and that some girls have real problems with their parents which are a lot bigger than just being shoved off the phone after an hour.

She's right, I suppose. But still.

TUESDAY

Still raining! I wonder is this one of the many dreadful results of global warming? I said this at the breakfast table this morning and Rachel said, 'Yeah, Rebecca, it's raining for two days in a row. In Ireland. How amazing. It must be the end of the world.'

She wouldn't joke about it if she had to sit in Miss Kelly's class. At least when the second ice age starts I will be prepared. Dad backed me up and said that global warming was something everyone should take seriously, and that it's up to all of us to do our bit to protect our green heritage. And then he went off to work in his petrol-eating, environment-wrecking car! He could just get the bus, seeing as the college is in the middle of town. Or he could walk, if he was feeling energetic. I mean, I have to walk to school every day, even when it rains. He'd only have an extra two miles to go. I'd walk three miles a day if it meant putting off the second ice age.

Although I wish I hadn't bothered walking to school at all today (not that I had a choice in the matter), because it was terrible. I mean, it's not usually a barrel of laughs, but it was particularly terrible today. I now have a new enemy. Well, actually, she's my first ever enemy, but whatever. She's our new English teacher, Mrs Harrington. We had our first English class today, and I was quite looking forward to it because I like English and I liked our old teacher Miss Ardagh (and not just because she always gave me good marks for essays). But she's gone off to write a book (which is pretty cool, I suppose, for an English teacher) and the new one is ... well.

It started when she was calling the roll. I was gazing out the window thinking about what I'd wear if we got another No Uniform Day this term when I heard my name. I said 'here' and looked out the window again, assuming she'd go straight on to Clare Reading who comes after me in the roll. But she didn't. She paused, and then she said,

'Rebecca Rafferty ... are you Rosie Carberry's daughter?'

I stared at her and said, 'Um, yeah.' And then I looked back down at my desk. Everyone knows that my mum is a writer, of course, and some girls in the class used to joke about it last year, but they all got sick of it pretty quickly and I certainly never mention it. The teachers all know too, but none of them have ever mentioned it either, apart from when Mrs Quinn asked me to get Mum to sign a book for her mother who was sick (Mrs Quinn's mother, of course, not my gran).

Anyway, I assumed that Mrs Harrington would just go on with the roll. But she didn't. She grinned at me in a mad way and said, 'I just love your mammy's books! I'm a big fan. That's how I recognised your name – I'd read about you in her interviews. She's very proud of you and your sister, isn't she? Now, what's your sister's name ... Rachel, isn't it?'

I just looked at her in horror. But she didn't care, because she is a scary stalker who probably has a special secret room covered in pictures of my mother. She just kept waffling on about my 'mammy's wonderful stories' and how *The Country Garden* was her favourite book of all time. And then she said, 'And I'm sure little Katie and Róisín are based on you and your big sister.'

Well, I'd been too horrified to speak until now, but I couldn't let that one go by.

'No,' I said. 'My mother never uses us in her books. Ever.' Besides, little Katie and Róisín were Irish-dancing champions and had ringlets. Urgh. Even the thought of having anything to do with those revolting freaks made me shudder.

Mrs Harrington, on the other hand, laughed.

'Oh, I'm sure there's a bit of you in that little Katie! You look very light on your feet.'

And I was so appalled by this that I literally couldn't speak.

I didn't want to have to say anything else to Mrs Harrington, but I did want to tell her that we never call Mum 'Mammy'. (I call her 'Mother' or 'Mother dear' when I'm annoyed with her.) Anyway, Mrs Harrington kept going on about how she hoped I'd inherited my mother's literary gifts while my so-called friends all sniggered behind their brand new copies of *Great Expectations*, which we are doing for our Junior Cert. Thank God no teacher went on like this last year when I was brand new to the school and didn't know anyone but Alice or I'd probably have no friends at all by now (apart from Alice. I hope). Mrs Harrington eventually remembered that this was meant to be an English class rather than a Rosie Carberry book-club meeting, but when the class was over, and I was trying to escape from the classroom as fast as I could, she pounced on me and said she had high hopes of getting some 'lovely essays from your mammy's daughter!'

I can't take a whole year (or five – oh God, we could have her every year until we leave!) of references to 'mammy's lovely books'. She wouldn't think they were so lovely if she'd heard the way my mum swears every time she realises she has to rewrite something.

WEDNESDAY ✿

Went to Cass's after school today. I love going over there; they always have nicer bread than we do. And Cass's room is much cooler than mine. I really, really want to redecorate my room but Mum and Dad say that I can't because I only got it done two years ago. As I was twelve then, it is hideous and pink and purple and not cool in any way, shape or form. Cass did her room up this year and it's brilliant. She has a cool sort of sixties' lamp and bedside rug from Urban Outfitters. I can't begrudge her the nice room, though, because she is my friend and she deserves a nice lamp (although so do I, and I don't have one.). We lay on the rug and had a very deep conversation about Life and What We Want to Do When We Grow Up (Me: Famous artist/actress. Cass: Theatre-set designer. This is a bit mysterious because it's not like Cass even goes to the theatre very often so I'm not sure why she feels so strongly about designing sets, but there you go) which gradually turned into a conversation about which teachers were the maddest, during which I announced that I hated Mrs Harrington with all my heart. She is getting worse by the day.

Cass said, 'I hate her too. I wish she'd stop going on about your "mammy".'

'Did you hear what she said today?' I said. "Oooh, you can tell you're your mammy's daughter, can't you? Such a way with words!".'

Cass said, 'She's sickening.'

'I know,' I said. 'She's my enemy. I think she's turning the class against me!'

'Oh, come on,' said Cass. 'She can't do that. It's not like anyone even likes her, and people like you.'

'She can,' I said. 'Ellie O'Mahony made some stupid joke about me being a 'mammy's girl' at lunch today. I mean, Ellie! What has she got against me all of a sudden? I thought we were friends. And anyway, she's a fine one to talk about mammies.' Ellie's mother is a total hippie. She became a hippie in the eighties, when being a hippie was not very fashionable. But Ellie's mum doesn't care. She has kept on with her hippiness. Some of it has now become accepted by the rest of the world – recycling, making stuff, growing veggies – so it seems that she was right all along. In some things. But not in others. She wears a lot of paisley and fabrics that she has handwoven herself (that wouldn't be quite as bad if she was any good at weaving, but she isn't), and she plays the lute, and she holds rituals to praise the Earth goddess every spring in their back garden. And Ellie's name is actually Galadriel, after the elf queen in *The Lord of the Rings* (only a few people at school know this), and she spent most of her childhood dressed like someone from Middle Earth. So as you can see, her mocking me for having an embarrassing mother is a bit much.

'Aw, I know it's bad, but I wouldn't worry too much about it,' said Cass. 'Ellie was only joking. I think it'll blow over. The novelty will have to wear off. And no one will really blame you for the way that stupid loon goes on.'

But I'm not so sure. They might think I'm encouraging her. They might think I actually like the attention. They might think I've always wanted people to make a fuss of me because of what Mum does. They might think I really am like the horrible children in her books.

I came home from Cass's and found my mother (source of all my woes) sitting at the kitchen table with a book and a glass of red wine. That's the second time she's been drinking wine this week. I hope she isn't turning into an alcoholic. Lots of writers are, I believe. Anyway, she shouldn't be carousing in the kitchen, she should be working on her next book. Her new one, *The Girl from Braddon Hall*, has been out for months and her agent Jocasta always says that she should start her next book before the new book comes out, because once the new book is out there'll be so much fuss and interviews and stuff it'll be harder to get started on a new story. And usually Mum starts writing the next book practically the day after she's finished the last one. But I don't think my mum has started a new project yet, because whenever she starts something new she always goes on and on about her new plot ideas and sometimes she tests them out on me and Rachel by telling us about them while we're making the dinner. But she hasn't mentioned any new story ideas since she finished going through the *Braddon Hall* proofs months and months ago. I pointed this out to her and she just laughed and said there was nothing to worry about.

'I hope that wasn't a drunken laugh,' I said, and left her to her lonely alcoholic revels. I met Dad on my way out of the kitchen. He was brandishing a wine glass of his own. Drinking on a Thursday night! At their age! Sometimes I think I'm the only sensible person in this house.

FRIDAY ☆

Brilliant day! First of all, school was okay – Mrs Harrington only mentioned my 'mammy' once, and only briefly.

We were hanging around with Ellie and Emma at lunch and Ellie was saying how much she hated Mrs Harrington, and it wasn't just because she'd found Ellie and Emma having a nice quiet game of Hangman when they were meant to be listening to the worst teacher ever waffle on about Wordsworth and his crazed daffodil obsession. It was also because Mrs Harrington was making my life a misery with her constant 'mammy'-ing. So I suppose Ellie isn't my enemy after all.

Then after school Alice and Cass came over to eat Chinese food from the De-Luxe takeaway and then stay the night. Mum and Dad left the house really early because they were going out for dinner somewhere in Meath, so we had the house to ourselves. Well, except for Rachel, who was there until seven and was then going out with Tom, the boyfriend she nearly went to Glastonbury with until my parents put their foot down and said she was far too young to go off to a festival in another country with just her eighteen-year-old boyfriend for company. For someone who nearly did all that, Rachel is very straightlaced when it comes to my welfare. She gave us this big lecture on 'not taking advantage of the free gaff' and how we weren't 'to throw a big party and drain Mum and Dad's drinks' cabinet'.

I said, 'Come on, Rachel, they're coming back at midnight, we're hardly going to have a big party.'

'Then why are you all dressed up, then?' said Rachel. She's so suspicious. She's worse than our parents, and she's only sixteen.

'Oh, I'm sorry,' I said. 'I suppose we should wear our school uniforms even when we're not in school, should we? Or sacks?'

Rachel sighed, in an annoying way. 'Don't break anything,' she said, and then she went off to meet Tom.

She's such a cow. We weren't dressed up at all. I was wearing jeans and a t-shirt and my favourite pink Converse, which is hardly fancy. Although I had put on some mascara and nicked some of Rachel's nice new lipgloss before she put her make-up bag in her handbag. . And it's not as if we could have had a proper party anyway, we don't know any boys and I can't imagine any of our school friends would be able to just come round to my house at the last minute. Anyway, we ordered a lovely feast from the takeaway and when the doorbell rang about twenty minutes later we were sure it was the food so I ran out to get it.

And standing on our doorstep was the best-looking boy I HAVE EVER SEEN IN REAL LIFE. I was so astounded I couldn't even speak. I just stared at him for what seemed like about ten years. The poor boy seemed slightly unsettled by this and we kind of stared at each other for a bit longer, until he said, 'Um, I'm from Smyth's the newsagent – I'm here to collect the paper money ...'

He was the new paperboy! We get the papers delivered at the weekends and the paperboy always comes around on Friday evenings to collect the money for them. But the paperboy didn't usually look like this. The usual paperboy is all squat and blotchy and wears a tracksuit. Paperboy II is tall and skinny with short, sort of curly dark brown hair and green eyes. Instead of a tracksuit, he was wearing really cool battered jeans and a nice band t-shirt. A gorgeous boy! On my doorstep!

Anyway, once he said who he was, I regained the power of speech and said, 'Oh, right, um, the money's round here somewhere ....' And while I was trying to think of something snappy and witty to follow that profound statement

Cass and Alice came out to the door, all 'where's our food?!' and 'come on, Bex, hand it over!' And then they too saw Paperboy and, like me, were STRUCK DUMB by his radiant beauty. I wonder does this happen to Paperboy all the time? It must make life rather awkward, if so. Anyway, luckily I noticed a fiver on the hall table next to a note from Mum which said 'MONEY FOR PAPERS' in large letters. So I gave the fiver to Paperboy and the three of us stared at him like love-struck loons as he counted out the change and gave it to me. I said, 'Thanks!' and he said, 'See you next week' (!!!!!) and I smiled and closed the door and then we ran into the sitting room and went 'squeeeeeeee!' And Alice said, in a very grand voice, 'I am in love.' Which was quite unexpected, because Alice is supposedly already in love with this bloke from St Anthony's Boys' School who goes past us on a bike every morning on Calderwood Road. She has fancied him for a year now, which is a long time to love someone you've never spoken to. But just one glimpse of the handsome paperboy was enough to make her forget the boy she has yearned for all year! Such is his power.

Anyway, I think Alice will have many rivals for

Paperboy's affections. Me and Cass, for example. And we have a big advantage, because we live around here, and Alice lives off near Kinsealy, far from Paperboy's paper round. In fact, Alice basically lives in the countryside. She used to live down the road from me on Glandore Road, but her family moved out to the wilds a few years ago. Her mum drops her near the top of my road on her way to work every morning and she walks to school with me and Cass, when we reach her road. So she will never see Paperboy unless she's in my house on a Friday evening. But neither Cass nor I pointed this out to her, because it might look like gloating.

Then the doorbell rang and for a split second I thought Paperboy might have come back because he was so smitten by our (or preferably just my) charms, but it was the Chinese food. Which was no substitute for Paperboy, but still, not bad. So we had a feast and we all kind of ate too much and felt a bit sick. But we recovered in time to watch our favourite old film, *Ten Things I Hate About You*, on DVD, which was brilliant even though none of the boys in it are vaguely as cute as Paperboy, our new love. Then we put on Beyoncé and danced on the couch, which was fun until

Cass fell off. Her glasses fell off in a different direction from the rest of her, and we couldn't find them for ages.

Now it's about one o'clock and the others have fallen asleep. Usually when we stay over in someone's house we stay up all night, but we're all exhausted tonight. I suppose it is the stress and strain of being back in school. And talking about Paperboy.

I wonder what his name is?

SUNDAY ◎

Went out to Alice's house. I wouldn't like to live so far away from town, but it's really gorgeous out there. We went for a walk (a proper country walk) and saw a fox and some rabbits, which was cool. The fox just ran out of a clump of bushes, stared at us, and ran back in again.

It was a lovely sunny day – no rain, hurrah – and it almost made me wish that I lived out among the wonders of nature instead of among three- and four-bedroom semi-detatcheds. We walked through this little bit of wood and it was all very pretty and peaceful. Alice isn't very observant, though. I kept seeing rabbits and squirrels and things, but every time Alice turned to look at them they had disappeared. Eventually she got cross (for Alice) and told me that she'd seen plenty of rabbits before and I didn't have to shriek like a banshee every time I saw one. I think she's just jealous because she lives out there right among the rural wildlife and keeps missing them when they emerge from their burrows, whereas I, the city slicker, could see them straight away. Maybe I will be a famous zoologist instead of a famous artist. I can present programmes on TV like David Attenborough, except younger. And a girl.

LATER

It just dawned on me now (because my mind is addled with love) that Paperboy must have actually delivered the papers to my house yesterday and this morning! How could we have been so stupid as to forget that important part of his job?! The very essence of his job, really. I can't believe he was actually on my doorstep again and I didn't ... well, actually, I suppose I couldn't have done anything.

It would have been a bit weird if I'd, like, suddenly opened the door as he was putting the papers in the letter box. Or even looked out at him through the letter box. Also, the papers are usually delivered before I wake up. But still. I could have looked out of Rachel's bedroom window.

MONDAY ❤

I am worried about my mother. I really, really don't think she's followed Jocasta's advice about starting a new book before the previous one is published. I mean, it's been months and months since the last one came out and every time I ask her whether she's started the new one she just gets a funny look on her face and says that 'everything's fine'. Which could mean anything! It could mean that she has writer's block and will never write again, which would make my life easier but not hers, and really, although Mum being a famous writer has a detrimental effect on my life (Mrs Harrington was in fine form today, I must say. She was 'mammy'-ing all over the place), she really does love writing and I don't want her to stop doing it. I know it sounds like I'm making a big deal over nothing but normally she likes going on about whatever she's writing at the moment. I've read that most writers hate this, but she doesn't. She says talking about her stories helps her work out any problems she has with them. So for her to be so secretive is very strange. I asked Dad what he thought, but he just laughed and said, 'Rebecca, your mum knows what she's doing. Don't worry.' I'm not sure she does, though. I think I have to keep an eye on her.

She does have this book party thing coming up soon, though, and her editor Lucy is coming over from London for it, so maybe she'll (Lucy, not Mum) be able to do something. This party is going to be very fancy. Mum's publishers are throwing it for her, to celebrate twenty years since her first book came out (and possibly to persuade her to actually write another one – surely Lucy and co must have realised this whole not-starting-a-new-book thing is a bit weird). Rachel and I will of course have to go – we always have to go to these things. They sound much more exciting than they actually are. We're usually the only people there under the age of thirty and if anyone bothers to talk to us at all they treat us as if we were about five. We end up hanging around the canapés (at the last book launch Rachel ate too many mini-burgers out of sheer boredom and Dad had to run to a chemist and get her some Gavis-con). So obviously I can't wait for this party. On the plus side, I might be able to emotionally blackmail Mum into letting me get some new clothes for it. But I wouldn't bet on it. She'll probably make me wear one of Rachel's old rags.

TUESDAY

Spent most of lunchtime with Cass and Alice, sitting in the corner of the junior cloakroom, talking about Paperboy. Well, actually, we mostly talked about whether we will ever get to take part in spontaneous synchronised dance routines. You know in films where one person starts doing a dance somewhere and then everyone joins in and before you know it there's a whole room full of people all doing the same dance? Both Cass and I dream of this happening to us but Alice says it would never happen in Ireland be-cause everyone here is far too repressed. She reminded us that the last time Mary's (the school down the road with the ridiculous stripey blazers) had one of their boring under-sixteens' discos back in May, it took about two hours before anyone plucked up the courage to move out onto the dance floor. You'd think we were all attached to the walls with magnets. By the time two brave Mary's girls got out on the dance floor and got the whole thing going, there was less than an hour of disco to go. We barely got to dance at all, let alone take part in a spontaneous synchronised dance session. And the music wasn't very good anyway. But Cass and I weren't in the mood for this sort of argument.

'Don't rain on our parade, Alice,' said Cass.

'Don't rain on our spontaneous dance routine, you mean,' I said. And we did a bit of spontaneous sitting-down-dancing just to annoy her. Sitting-down dancing can be quite fun. You just move the top half of yourself. We have worked out a few quite complex routines (we have to be prepared in case we ever get to start a spontaneous dance session) and we used to do it quite a lot last year, to liven up boring geography classes when Kelly had her back to the class. I think it helped relieve the tension caused by her terrifying accounts of floods and ice ages and stuff.

Alice got all cross. 'Right,' she said, 'suppose you did start a stupid dance. How would you feel if Paperboy came in and saw you doing it?'

'Delighted,' I said proudly. And I would. And surely so would he. Who wouldn't be impressed by a big spontaneous dance routine? Well, apart from Alice the killjoy, of course. And how cool would it be if Paperboy joined in the dancing? That would be the greatest thing ever, as I pointed out. Alice reluctantly agreed that that would indeed be pretty cool. Then we talked about Paperboy a bit more seriously. We can't figure a way of talking to him properly or even finding out his name without acting like pyschos. Why, why, why do we have to go to a poxy all-girls school? We wouldn't be plotting ways to follow paperboys around if we actually got to talk to any boys about anything other than the price of the *Irish Times*.

WEDNESDAY

Mrs Harrington was awful at school today. We have to do an essay for our English homework, and after she wrote the choice of titles on the blackboard she looked at me in a mad way and said, 'Now Miss Rafferty, I can't wait to see what you come up with! Something from you is the next best thing to a new Rosie Carberry book!' Maybe she thinks I am, like, the second coming of my mother? That is a terrifying thought on many different levels. And obviously my school essay will not be anything like my mother's awful books.

At home, I asked my mum again if she'd started her new book yet. She just laughed and went off to hide in her study. I am worried. I think she could be losing her mind. She's usually so hard-working. I asked Rachel if she thought Mum was going mad and she laughed for about twenty-five minutes. When she was able to speak, she said, 'No, Bex, I don't think she's going mad. Just because she didn't tell you exactly what she's writing doesn't mean she's insane. Actually, I'm pretty sure she has started something new, she just doesn't want to tell us about it.'

I didn't know what to think of that, so I went in to surprise Mum in her study, to see if I could catch her writing. But, to my amazement, she was just sitting back in her chair reading *Kiss* and *Sugar*!!! She *never* reads my magazines. In fact, every time she sees them she goes on about how they're a waste of money and end up in the recycling the day I get them (just like her newspapers and grown-up magazines, as I have pointed out a million times, though of course she never seems to see any similarities). I asked her what she was doing and she jumped about ten feet in the air and told me not to sneak in like that. And she wouldn't answer my question about why she was reading the magazines. She just told me to go and do my homework and stop annoying her.

What can this mean?!?

LATER

I just realised that Mum was reading the new issues of those magazines. I'd seen them in the shops but I hadn't even bought either of them yet. Which means SHE BOUGHT THEM HERSELF! What is going on?!

THURSDAY ☾

Told Cass and Alice about Mum's strange behaviour. They were very sympathetic, but I don't feel very comforted. Alice said it sounded like Mum was going through some sort of mid-life crisis and was trying to recapture her lost youth. I don't like the sound of that. Maybe she's going to start wearing 'cool' clothes and going out to clubs till the small hours of the morning. She might bring Dad along with her! Oh, God, I really, really hope she isn't having a crisis. I don't think I could bear the shame. She went over to her friend Gemma's house tonight but she was dressed pretty normally (for a forty-five-year-old) so I don't think she was going out grooving. Although it's eleven o'clock and she's not back yet. So you never know. Maybe she's dancing on a table as I write.

LATER

Also, you'd think that if she wanted to recapture her lost youth she wouldn't want to recapture being fourteen. We can't even get into clubs. She should be trying to be about twenty and start reading, like, *Cosmo* and stuff.

SATURDAY ★

Saw Paperboy again last night! And he spoke to me about something other than papers! I am very happy, even though Rachel is being really, really annoying. She kept asking me why I'd changed out of my school uniform so quickly and why I was wearing the pink bead necklace Alice got me in Berlin for my birthday. I wasn't dressed up or anything, I was just wearing my little Sleater-Kinney t-shirt with a cat on it and my nice dark jeans, so I don't know why she had to make such a big deal out of it. Anyway, we had just finished dinner when the doorbell rang and I practically knocked my chair over getting out to the hall first. And then I opened the door and there he was!

Paperboy! And he was just as gorgeous as ever! I smiled at him and said, 'Hi,' and he smiled back and said, 'Hi, I'm here for the paper money.' He's got a lovely voice; it's all sort of scratchy. I wonder how old he is? He doesn't look much older than me. Anyway, I said I'd get the money and went in to the kitchen to get it off Mum, and Rachel was standing there with this horrible grin on her face. She kept smirking at me while Mum got the money out of her wallet, until finally I couldn't stand it anymore and shouted, 'What?!' and she was all, 'Nothing, nothing.' I hate her.

So I got the money off Mum and went back to the hall (Rachel followed me out just to annoy me more) and gave it to Paperboy and he said, 'Thanks' and I said, 'You're welcome', and he turned to go. He'd taken a few steps down the drive and I was just closing the door when he turned around and said, 'Cool t-shirt, by the way.' And I was so astonished I didn't know what to say so I just gawped at him and finally said, 'Um, I got it on the Internet' which was a very boring thing to say. I should have thought of some witty retort, or at least said something cool like, 'Oh, I just picked it up in New York last month.'

Although that would have been a lie, and he might have started talking to me about New York, and I would have to admit that I'd never been there and he'd think I was mad. Anyway, he sort of went 'oh, right' and then he waved and went off to his bike and the rest of his paper round. I closed the door in a state of bliss which vanished when I turned around and saw Rachel standing there with a very, very irritating expression on her stupid face.

'Oh my God, you so fancy him,' she said.

'No I don't,' I said. 'He has excellent taste in t-shirts, that's all.'

'Huh,' said Rachel. 'No wonder you're all dressed up.'

'Oh, shut up,' I said. 'You're just jealous because he said something nice to me and ignored you.'

'He couldn't see me!' said Rachel, before she remembered that she was too old and snotty to take her little sister seriously and said in this very patronising voice, 'I think it's great, anyway. It's nice for you to have a boy who isn't a fictional character to think about for a change.'

And then she ran up the stairs before I could leap on her in a fit of rage and kill her, which is what I wanted to do. But my rage quickly subsided because PAPERBOY

TOLD ME HE LIKES MY T-SHIRT! I rang Cass and told her what had happened.

I felt a bit guilty telling her what Paperboy said about my t-shirt in case she thought I was gloating. She was a bit quiet when I told her about it. I hope our love for Paperboy doesn't come between us. I don't think it will because we're not stupid and we know what friends are more important than boys (even very, very cute boys in olive-green Converse), but passionate love makes people do strange things.

SUNDAY

Rachel is driving me mad. She's acting like she's a twenty-five-year-old woman of the world who knows everything about love, not a sixteen-year-old who's been going out with her very first boyfriend for six months. She keeps following me around the house and asking me do I want to talk to her about anything. Which I don't. And even if I did, I wouldn't, because I don't want to give her the satisfaction of watching me come to her for advice. Which is something I will never, ever do.

Except when I went to her about Mum last week. But that was different. I will never, ever go to her for love advice.

LATER

Although she really is more experienced in the ways of love than any of my friends.

LATER

But she is also much more annoying.

MONDAY ❤

I'm writing this in history. It is very, very boring. We are doing the Reformation and have to write about what it would have been like to hear Martin Luther preach in the 1520s. I can only imagine that listening to him going on about reading the Bible in German was just as boring as this class. To amuse myself I have drawn a picture of Cass as a turnip-eating sixteenth-century peasant at the back of my copy book. I just showed it to her and she has written a note on it saying 'Why is your self-portrait wearing my glasses?' Huh.

Anyway. Me and Cass and Alice were a bit late for class so we couldn't sit together. I am sitting next to Vanessa Finn. She is very annoying. I mean, she's not particularly annoying at the moment, because she's just sitting there staring blankly at pictures of popes in the history book, but in general she is annoying. So is her best friend Caroline. Vanessa never shuts up about how terrible it is for her having to go to a state school and Caroline just nods sympathetically. They never do any spontaneous dancing; they just talk about hair and about all the things Vanessa buys when she makes her weekly trek over to the Dundrum shopping centre and pretends she's from the southside. Alice, Cass and I never talk about hair, partly because our own hair is just too depressing to talk about. Well, mine and Cass's is. Mine is boring, brown and wavy. That sounds okay, but it always looks a bit mad. It doesn't respond well to damp weather so most of the time I have to tie it back or it just gets bigger and bigger as the day goes on. Cass's hair is also wavy and sort of golden brown and would be okay if it wasn't taking about ten years to grow out her fringe. She has had a sort of fringe for as long as I've known her (a year), but apparently she got it cut when she was about eleven and has been trying to grow it out ever since. But every time she goes to the hairdresser the hairdresser trims the end bits 'to frame her face' so she can never get rid of it. In fact, the only one who has nice hair is Alice. She has shiny, well-behaved proper golden blonde hair, the sort of hair no one really has in Ireland unless they dye it. This is because her mum is German and incredibly blonde. Alice's mum came over here in the eighties when she was a student and for some weird reason she loved Ireland so much she couldn't bear to leave. She says she thought Ireland was a magical place and by the time she realised it wasn't she had made lots of friends here and had got together with Alice's dad so she liked it anyway. Alice can speak German perfectly. The first time I heard her talking to her mum 'auf Deutsch' (as they say) it was really weird – it sounded so strange to hear perfect German coming out of ordinary old Alice. But there you are.

Alice doesn't do German at school, even though she would get all As if she did, because as far as I can tell her German is better than our teacher's. She certainly sounds properly German, whereas Frau O'Hara sounds like someone from Cork who just happens to be speaking German, which is basically what she is. But anyway, Alice thought doing German with a bunch of halfwits like me, who take two weeks to learn how to ask for directions to a youth hostel, would give her an unfair advantage so she did French instead. This is because she is a good person (or possibly mad). I, of course, am not good at all and if my mother was German there is absolutely no way I'd have done French. This is why Alice is a better person than me. Every so often she offers to help me practise German conversation. I always say no, mostly because I know it's because she's heard me speaking German and knows how bad my German is. She just feels sorry for me. Cass (who does Spanish) says I'm being silly and should take advantage of having a special tutor but it's actually embarrassing talking so badly in a language to someone who speaks it properly (I don't think Frau O'Hara notices, her own German is pretty awful. According to Alice, of course. I'm hardly one to judge).

TUESDAY ☼

Today for the first time this term Miss Kelly actually did proper normal geography instead of telling us about the end of the world. I never thought I'd say this, but it was kind of a relief just to listen to her waffle on about the Ruhrgebiet and the sorry state of German industry in general. All those long descriptions of tidal waves crashing over Dublin and killing us all were freaking me out. Also, I was secretly getting afraid that she was never going to teach us anything on the course and we would all fail our Junior Cert. I mean, I always welcome anything that can distract a teacher from the actual class (which is why we always try to get Mrs O'Reilly to tell us about the time she was visiting an ancient amphitheatre and her husband fell down the steps and into a lion pit). But Kelly hasn't actually done anything on the course since January. Our summer tests were all about greenhouse gasses (we all got As). But sadly, the end of the world is not going to be on our Junior Cert exam. I mean, I don't care about geography, but I don't actually want to fail it or anything. It was even too much for Cass, who always manages to get As without doing any work at all and who is always the first to get O'Reilly onto the subject of Roman steps and how very, very slippy they were.

WEDNESDAY ✿

Kelly told us about French rivers today. I started falling asleep until Cass kicked me.

THURSDAY ☾

Oh my God, I would give anything for Miss Kelly to tell us about mile-high tidal waves. Anything! She's been talking about EU livestock quotas for forty minutes.

LATER

I have decided that Mum needs my help to get over this

terrible writer's block. I mentioned this to Rachel this evening and she laughed. I'm glad she finds me so amusing. When I've single-handedly saved our mother's career she'll be sorry. Of course, I'm just not sure how I'm going to do it yet. But I'll come with something. God knows my life is so boring I have plenty of time to use my imagination. It seems as though all bestselling books for grown-ups include three women who are meant to be very different but are all the same really (their hair is usually different colours, but that's about it) and how their friendship supports them through the hard times. And as it is a book by my mum, then there will have to be a devoted mammy who dispenses wisdom to her daughters (very unlike my own mother, I must say). I could even write it myself, actually. How hard could writing a book be?

FRIDAY ✯

Miss Kelly seems to have reached a compromise. She did boring geography for about half an hour and then gave us a passionate lecture on the evils of not washing everything we put into the green recycling bin. It's nice to have her back. Well, not nice, exactly, because she's always a bit scary and sometimes when she's been particularly extreme I have nightmares about the end of the world, but it's better than learning about the GDP of Belgium.

Called in to Cass's after school. Alice couldn't come because her guitar teacher was sick on Tuesday, when she normally has classes, and she had to switch days. Alice is quite good at the guitar, but she's learning classical guitar so she doesn't have an electric one, just an acoustic one with big plastic strings. She can play some cool stuff on it anyway. Apparently her dad has an electric one somewhere but it doesn't have an amplifier so it's no use. Anyway, Cass's brother is so annoying. We were in her room trying to have a serious conversation (well, sort of. Actually, Cass was telling me about her recurring dream in which Miss Kelly has challenged her to a duel like in days of old, and Cass only has twenty-four hours to learn how to use a sword. She doesn't know what on earth this means. Neither do I, although I did have a few theories, mostly about global warming). But Nick kept coming in saying stupid and usually disgusting things like, 'Did you know the human body is 90% snot?' (which isn't even true THANK GOD). He is *so* irritating. He actually makes me grateful for Rachel, and I never thought I'd say that.

MONDAY ♥

My plan to inspire my poor, suffering mother has begun. I spent today thinking of excellent plots for her (it was a nice distraction from my classes, which were very, very boring) and have begun to work them casually into conversation in the hope that it will inspire Mum's creative powers. Although frankly I think I have done nearly all the creating myself already. I've practically written four books today (in my head). I began putting the plan into action when I was helping Mum make the dinner, peeling potatoes like a slave (what would Mrs Harrington say if she knew her beloved Rosie Carberry used child labour in the home?). Mum was messing around with a big orange casserole dish and saying something boring about not cutting off half the potato when I got rid of the purply bits when I said, 'You know, Mum, I heard a very interesting thing at school today.'

'Oh really?' said Mum. 'Was it more interesting than peeling those potatoes properly?'

'Yes,' I said. 'A girl in my class was telling us about her aunt. Apparently she had two really good friends, right, and they all went to school together but when they got older one of them became a teacher, and she was really bored and frustrated because she had to teach girls about tidal waves all day, and then another of them ran a fancy hotel, and she met all these glamorous men who were staying in the hotel, and the last one was a nurse and she was very saintly.'

'Really,' said my mother. 'Which one was your friend's aunt?'

'Um,' I said. 'The nurse. No, sorry, the teacher. Anyway, over the years they all went their separate ways, and then they met up again and shared their stories. Oh, and they went on holiday together and the nurse found love for the first time. And the teacher learned to follow her dreams and see all the places she'd taught classes about.'

'Fascinating,' said Mum. 'What about the hotel manager?'

'She decided she liked just, like, flirting with all the men in the hotel. So she was pretty happy.'

'Wow,' said Mum. 'That's quite a story.'

'Well,' I said. 'Just thought you'd be interested.' And I gave her a meaningful look. But she wasn't looking at me. She was sort of looking off into the distance with a funny expression on her face. Could I have inspired her already?

TUESDAY

I don't think I have inspired Mum. I heard her on the phone to Joscasta this evening. First of all she was laughing in a sort of mad sniggering way. Why doesn't she ever laugh like a normal person when she's on the phone? She sounds like a horse. Maybe she has a special phone laugh like some people have a special posh phone voice. Although you'd think if she went to the trouble of coming up with a phone laugh she wouldn't sound like a farm animal. Then she was saying 'no, Jocasta, they don't know. It's not a big deal!' Then she saw the door into the sitting room was open and went upstairs to her and Dad's room so I couldn't hear anything else. What is she going on about now?

Could she be sick?

I am a bit worried.

WEDNESDAY ✿

This evening I sort of cornered Dad when he was making the risotto and hissed, 'Dad, do you know what's wrong with Mum? Why isn't she writing her new book?'

Dad sort of looked at me and then he said, 'Bex, are you really, seriously worried about this?'

'Yes!' I said. 'I'm worried she won't be able to write any more and then she'll be miserable and ...'

And then, to my shame, I burst into tears. Dad was very nice and even though normally these days whenever either of my parents try to hug me I just go 'gerrof' and escape from their annoying clutches as fast as I can, I didn't actually mind being hugged this time. He told me seriously not to worry and that Mum didn't have writer's block and that soon she would have a nice surprise for all of us. 'Especially nice for you,' he said, which cheered me up a bit. Maybe Mum is writing a film, and maybe there will be a part for me! Or maybe one of her books is being made into a film, and someone really famous and cool is going to be in it. I'm quite looking forward to the stupid book party now.

THURSDAY ☾

It's Mum's book party tomorrow and she still hasn't started a new book. At least, if she has, she's not telling us about it, which just isn't like her at all. She's off at the shops now, looking for a bag to go with her book-launch dress. I really am worried about her, although Rachel pointed out (in quite a kind way, really, not her usual horrible, patronising way) that if Mum really was suffering from writer's block, she wouldn't be so cheerful. She'd be sobbing and wailing in frustration, according to Rachel. I couldn't imagine Mum wailing, and it wasn't a very nice thought, but I suppose Rachel is right about the writer's block thing.

'But then what do you think is wrong?' I asked.

'I don't think anything's wrong,' said Rachel. 'Seriously, I think she's working on something. She's in her study every morning, as usual. And she seems fine.'

'But if she's working on something, why won't she tell us?' I said.

'Maybe it's something she doesn't want to tell us about,' said Rachel. 'Maybe she's changing direction.' She stopped, and suddenly looked a bit sick. 'Oh, God, Bex, maybe she's writing, like, really sexy stuff.' She stared at me in horror, and I stared back. 'Maybe she's writing a big sexy blockbuster. Like Louise Bagshawe, Jilly Cooper or Jackie Collins or something. That's ... that's practically porn!'

'What?!' I said. What a horrible thought! It's bad enough having a mother who writes about feisty Irish mammies and their roguish children, but having a mother who wrote porn would be a zillion times worse. I could never, ever live it down.

'Oh God,' said Rachel. 'The shame. And we can't ever read it. We'd keep imagining ... urrrrrgh. It'll traumatise us for life.'

'No wonder she hasn't told us anything,' I said, sitting on the couch. 'Oh, God, I feel sick.'

'I feel sicker,' said Rachel. She sat down next to me.

'Should we ask her about it again?' I said.

'Oh, for goodness sake, Bex, we've both tried that,' said

Rachel in an exasperated way. So she *had* asked Mum about her new project! I knew she thought the whole thing was freaky! And there she was telling me I was over-reacting. 'She's not going to suddenly tell us anything now.'

Then the phone rang. We both jumped about ten feet in the air – I think we both thought it was Mum ringing to remind us to put the casserole in the oven for dinner. But it was Tom for Rachel. She's on the phone to him now, talking in her Tom-phone-voice, which is absolutely sickening. At least she has a boyfriend to comfort her about having a pornographer for a mother. I don't even have a Cass and an Alice because they're both out at the cinema tonight (I didn't go because they're going to see a scary film and I can't watch scary films in the cinema. In fact, I can't really watch scary films at all unless I'm watching them from the sitting-room door so I can leap back into the hall if anything gross happens). At least I'll get to see my future love, Paperboy, tomorrow, though.

FIVE MINUTES LATER

Except I won't, because I'll be at that stupid book party!

My mother is wrecking my entire life!

SATURDAY ★

BESTSELLER DISCOVERS NEW DIRECTION

Rosie Carberry is set to win a whole new generation of fans with the publication of her first book for teenagers. May the Best Girl Win *is flagged to become a Christmas bestseller. Rosie is the mother of two teenage daughters, 16-year-old Rachel and 14-year-old Rebecca, and says the story was inspired by their antics.*

Antics. ANTICS! I don't have antics! Or make antics. Whatever. I hate my mother. I can't believe I was trying to help break her writer's block. I'd rather she had writer's block forever and ever if this is what she's going to come out with. A teen novel! Officially inspired by my 'antics'!!! I can't believe she has done this to me. I will never, ever live this down. I thought Mrs Harrington was bad enough, comparing me with those horrible little ringleted loons.

But now my evil mother has admitted to the world that she has based a character on me! And Rachel too, but it turns out that Ruthie O'Reilly (that's the heroine of this hideous monstrosity of a book) is fourteen, which means everyone will just think it's me anyway.

Anyway. As you can tell from that newspaper report, which I have stuck in this diary just to prove that last night wasn't all a hideous dream, Mum had a lovely surprise for us at the book party. In fact, it turned out that the party wasn't just to celebrate her twenty years as a published writer. It was also to celebrate her 'new venture into the exciting world of young adult literature'. At least, that's what it said in today's *Irish Times*.

Last night was the worst night of my entire life. And today is looking like being the worst day. It started with me opening the door in my pyjamas to find Paperboy standing just outside it (the door, that is, not my 'jamas). I was letting out our cat Bumpers, who hates going to the toilet in his litter tray like a normal cat and always demands to leave the house first thing in the morning, and I was still in such a daze after last night that I forgot it was Saturday, the only day we get the papers delivered. So when I saw Paperboy standing about six inches away from me with some papers in his hand I actually shrieked. And then I stepped back and stood on Bumpers, and Bumpers shrieked too and ran out the door and between Paperboy's ankles. It was like something out of a very, very crap circus.

And of course the door suddenly opening and me shrieking (with my hair sticking up all over the place, I might add) and a cat wailing and practically running him over gave Paperboy a hideous fright, so he yelled and fell off the step. And he dropped a whole pile of papers and bits of them fell all over the place and on one of the pages was a huge colour photo of me. Well, me with Mum and Rachel anyway. On the third page of the *Irish Times*. We were sort of grimacing at the camera and Mum was beaming from ear to ear like a lunatic. I was so horrified by this I forgot to say sorry to Paperboy for scaring him. In fact, I nearly shrieked again. Unfortunately Paperboy, who was picking up the papers and putting them back in his bag, noticed what I was staring at and said, 'Hey ... sorry for giving you a fright. Is, um, is that you?'

'Is that me where?' I said, idiotically.

'On this paper,' said Paperboy, helpfully picking it up

and holding it out to me so I could see myself and my evil traitorous mother in glorious technicolour. 'And ... this one.' He held up a copy of the *Irish Independent* which had fallen to bits. On one of the pages that had dropped out was a huge photo of me and Mum. I can't describe the freakish expression on my face in that photo. It was too hideous for words.

'Oh God,' I said.

'I thought I recognised you,' said Paperboy, sticking the last of his papers into the bag. And he grinned at me. 'See you!' he said. Then he went off. And I was left, standing there, staring after him like a pyjama-wearing freak. And now I am hiding in my room. I am never coming out again. Mum keeps knocking at my door and saying, 'Oh come on, Bex, you've got to eat some time'. She's right, actually, I'm starving, but I'm not going to eat any of her horrible food. I'll go out and buy my own.

FIVE MINUTES LATER

Except all my money (such as it is) was given to me by her and Dad (who is just as bad as her, I might add, because of course it turns out he knew about her evil book all the time!). So technically it would still be their food. Huh.

To distract myself from my agonising hunger, I will finally write about what happened last night, aka the worst night of my life. Mum was all flustered and frantic beforehand, which isn't like her at all really, although of course now I know that it was her GUILTY CONSCIENCE because she knew what was coming. Rachel and I got dressed up, and the gorgeous Topshop dress I got for my birthday and haven't had the chance to wear much yet actually looked really nice and my hair was behaving itself for some miraculous reason (probably because when I was washing my hair yesterday I nicked Mum's expensive Bumble and Bumble conditioner that she keeps hidden under her bed). So I actually felt quite good when we left the house. But little did I know the hideous nightmare that awaited me. We arrived at the hotel (oh yeah, the publishers had rented a really gorgeous room in a posh hotel) and there was Lucy who edits Mum's books at the publisher and Mum's agent Jocasta and lots of journalists and friends of Mum. In other words, it was the usual rubbish. There were photographers and we had to pose for a few photos with Mum (we didn't know then where they would end up). Rachel and I had to be polite and say hello to people, and a waiter was handing around champagne and Rachel asked if she could have a glass and Mum said no, maybe later if there were toasts, and then Rachel asked if she could have a glass of wine and Mum said no again, so me and Rachel sort of skulked off and hid behind a pillar where hopefully no one would notice us and start talking to us about Mum's books.

'God, this is boring,' said Rachel, looking at her watch. 'I wonder how soon we can leave.'

'Not for hours and hours,' I said gloomily. 'Are there any mini-burgers left?' Mini-burgers are the only good thing about these launches. For some reason they are nicer than ordinary-sized burgers. Why? Who knows? I thought eating a few of them would ease my pain, but even that pleasure was denied me.

'No,' said Rachel. 'I just saw Dad eat the last one. Oh, look, I think Lucy's going to say something now.'

'Great,' I said. 'Speeches. My favourite things.'

Little did I know how bad this particular speech was going to be.

It started in the usual way – Lucy went on about Mum's brilliant career and the contribution she'd made to Irish writing, and how she was one of the first international Irish bestselling authors (a slight exaggeration – if she was really such an international bestseller, we wouldn't live in a three-bedroom semi in Drumcondra; we'd live in some sort of palace in Killiney. Not that I'd want to live in Killiney, but I wouldn't mind having a bigger house. And a view of the sea would be nice. Although I suppose I could get that in, like, Clontarf or somewhere. Anyway.). So this went on for a while, and I sort of drifted off and was gazing longingly at a tray of mini-burgers that had suddenly appeared on the other side of the room when Lucy said, 'But of course, the real reason we're here tonight is to launch a new stage in Rosie's career. As most of you know, her new book will be aimed at a whole new audience – teenagers!'

I wish I could say that everyone gasped in horror, but that was just me and Rachel. In fact, everyone else seemed to know all about it and nodded sagely while Rachel and I stared at each other.

'As you know, Rosie has two lovely teenage daughters

and she thought it would be a good idea to write something that they and their friends could enjoy.' (FYI, I can safely say that I – and my friends, for that matter – will never enjoy anything written by my mother.) 'All of us at Peregrine have heard a lot about Rachel and Rebecca over the years, and about a year ago we were delighted when Rosie told us she wanted to write something inspired by their adventures. And we weren't disappointed. *May the Best Girl Win* will be the highlight of our children's list this season!' And she held up a copy of a stupid-looking book with a horrible drawing of a pouty girl in Ugg boots on the cover. I thought I was going to be sick.

Then Mum took the microphone. She carefully avoided looking at us, probably because even she wouldn't have the cheek to waffle on about her awful book while Rachel and I glowered at her. She thanked Lucy and then she thanked her publishers and her editor and her agent and everyone for coming to the event and just when I thought I was going to faint from a combination of boredom and rage she said, 'And of course, thanks most of all to my family – my husband Ed and my lovely daughters, Rachel and Rebecca. Those girls drive me mad sometimes,' (and of course everyone laughed like this was funny) 'but I don't know what Ed and I would do without them. They make us laugh a lot.'

Everyone sort of went 'awww' and of course turned around to gawp at us and see how we were taking this touching speech. I think they thought we'd be wiping away tears of emotion and mouthing 'we love you!' at our awful horrible sneaking mother. But we weren't, we were just standing there glaring at her.

Mum cleared her throat and went on. 'The girls aren't really fans of my books – I think it was Rebecca who described the last one as 'nice if you like that sort of thing' – so I decided to write a book they would really like, about their world.'

Oh my God, that's what it's all about! Punishment for mocking those evil Irish dancing children! The unfairness!

Mum kept waffling on. 'It's been a long time since I was a teenager,' (everyone laughed again as if this was a joke, when of course it is simply THE TRUTH) 'but I can remember what it was like, and of course I have Rachel and Rebecca around to remind me all the time. Their antics inspired me to write this book, although I had a little help from teen magazines. I think the girls wondered what I was doing with some of them!'

Yeah, I did. I can't believe I was worried about her having a mid-life crisis when she was really just getting ready to embarrass me in front of the world. I can't believe I actually CRIED the other night because I thought there was something wrong with her. I am never going to be nice to her again.

'But I really enjoyed writing the book,' she said. 'And I'm already working on the sequel. So, well, I hope you enjoy it!'

And everyone clapped. The fools. Soon they all started moving around chatting and eating canapés, but Rachel and I were still pretty much frozen to the spot.

'I can't believe it,' said Rachel. 'I can't believe I never guessed.'

'I can't believe she's been spying on us and planning to write a book without telling us!' I said.

'Yeah,' said Rachel. 'Bex, I think this is worse than the porn thing.'

Just then, my dad came up to us, beaming from ear to ear.

'Hi girls!' he said, as if his wife hadn't just DESTROYED OUR LIVES. 'What do you think?'

'You knew?' shrieked Rachel.

Dad looked confused. 'Of course I knew,' he said. 'What's wrong? Aren't you excited? I thought you'd be excited!'

'Of course we're not excited!' I said. 'Is this what you were talking about when you said Mum had a surprise and that I'd like it?

'Um, yes,' said Dad.

'Well I don't!' I cried.

'But why?' said Dad. He looked very confused, but then, he often does. It's what happens when you lock yourself away and teach history for twenty years.

'Because she's written a book and she's just told the world it's about us,' said Rachel. 'I mean, it's bad enough having that awful teacher going on about how we must love Mum's books every time I bump into her in the corridor, even though she isn't even my English teacher ...' (Ha! I knew Mrs Harrington wouldn't leave Rachel alone.) 'but now Mum's actually officially said that she's written about us. How do you expect us to be happy about that? It's humiliating!'

'It's worse for me,' I said. 'She's just said that this girl in the book is fourteen. So everyone will think it's about me.'

'Well, I was fourteen once too,' said Rachel. 'So that doesn't help much.'

'Girls!' said Dad. 'You're being very silly. I'm sorry you're upset, but I really don't see what the problem is. Your mum's very excited about this book and she's already working on the sequel. Last week you were convinced she had writer's block! You were crying, Bex!'

'I'd PREFER writer's block to an awful book about a girl in stupid hideous boots who everyone will think is me!'

'Oh God,' said Rachel. 'Everyone we know is going to read it if they think it's about us. It's going to be so embarrassing.'

And then our enemy, aka our mother, came over. She had a sort of stupid smile on her face.

'Well, girls,' she said. 'How did you like my surprise?'

'If by "how did you like my surprise?", you mean, 'How do you like being embarrassed in front of the whole world?' Well, the answer is "not at all"!' shouted Rachel, and can I just say how nice it was to see Rachel being all snotty to

Mum in front of me. Normally if she gets annoyed by Mum when I'm in the room, she tries to be all grown up and sophisticated, but as we don't live in a vast mansion and I am not deaf, I know perfectly well she can be just as tantrum-ish as me when she thinks I can't hear her. Which I always can.

Mum seemed genuinely confused.

'What's so embarrassing about this?' she said.

Rachel and I stared at her.

'Mother,' I said, very slowly, 'you have written a book that you have just admitted is inspired by us. And people we know will read it. HOW IS THAT NOT EMBARRASSING?'

'I hate to say this, Mum, but Bex is right,' said Rachel. 'Seriously, we are going to look like complete fools. I can't believe you've done this to us!'

'I thought you'd like it!' said Mum. 'You never want to read my books, so I thought you'd like this one.'

Against my will, I found myself feeling a bit sorry for her.

'And how do you know you'll be embarrassed?' she went on. 'You haven't even read it yet! It's fun! Your friends will like it!'

'I don't need to read it,' I said, 'to know that it will be embarrassing.' She looked genuinely confused and I started feeling a bit bad.

'But I thought ...' she started to say, but then one of her writing pals ran up.

'Rosie!' she cried. 'I can't believe it – I never thought you'd start writing for kids!' She looked at us in a patronising sort of way. 'Although I should have known you'd want to write something for your little ones.'

I stopped feeling bad for Mum then. And she must have realised that the looks on my and Rachel's faces meant we couldn't hold in our rage much longer.

'Hmm, yes,' she said. 'Hey, have you met Conor Hamilton? He's over there, come on ...' And she sort of moved the annoying friend away.

'I'm going home,' I said. 'Coming, Rachel?'

'Yeah,' said Rachel. Then we both kind of paused. 'Um,' said Rachel. 'Can we have bus fare, please? I didn't bring my wallet.'

'No you can't,' said Dad, sounding genuinely cross, which is rare for him. He hardly ever loses his temper. 'And

I can't believe you're acting like such silly babies. You're too old for this. Now, all your mother's friends and colleagues are here and I don't want you making a show of yourselves in front of them, it's not fair to her.'

'It's not fair to us, more like,' I muttered.

Dad glared at me. He's surprisingly good at glaring when he wants to. 'I understand you're a bit surprised,' he said. 'But that doesn't mean you have to act like a pair of five-year-olds. Okay?'

'Okay,' said Rachel, but she rolled her eyes so he would know she didn't mean it. 'Can I at least have a glass of wine?'

'No,' said Dad. 'Oh, all right. Just one. And NOT you,' he said, looking at me. Not that I wanted wine anyway. I'd probably start trying to drown my sorrows straight away and then I'd become an alcoholic. That'd give Mum something to write about, I suppose. A waiter came along with a tray of drinks, so Rachel took her wine and I took an orange juice and then we went and sat in a corner and ate canapés.

'Just look at her,' said Rachel. 'Look at her talking to her ridiculously dressed mates (seriously, what is that man wearing? Is that a velvet bow tie?) like she hasn't a care in the world.'

'She hasn't,' I said. 'She's not the one who's going to be publicly humiliated as soon as everyone she knows reads that stupid book.'

'I can't BELIEVE I was feeling sorry for her,' said Rachel. And we sat and glowered at her and tried to eat the canapés without getting bits of diced tomato all over ourselves (all the little tarts and things are surprisingly messy) until at LAST Dad took us home (Mum was staying on, probably so she didn't have to face us). And then I went to bed and woke up hoping it was all a horrible dream and ... well, you know the rest. So that's it.

I just rang Alice to tell her my troubles but she was at her mad auntie Fran's house and her mobile went straight to voicemail so I couldn't talk to her. And Cass was at her piano lesson so I couldn't get through to her either. I am both enraged and bored. What a terrible life I have. Also, I am still really, really hungry. But I don't want to go downstairs.

TWENTY MINUTES LATER

Mum just came to the door.

'Rebecca?'

'Go away,' I said. Was that toast I could smell? Does she have toast? Is she trying to lure me out with food?

'Look, I'm going to leave the book outside the door. I think you'll really like it. It's not really about you, seriously. No one will think it is.'

'Huh!' I said. I wish I could have come up with a more witty riposte, but in fairness I was practically dying of starvation.

I heard her go downstairs and then, I'll admit it, I opened the door. There was a copy of the stupid book with a plate of scrambled eggs on toast sitting on the top.

I took the whole lot inside and ate the eggs on toast in about two seconds. I felt a bit better after that. It seemed like I'd been starving for ages so I thought it must be about two o'clock at least but when I looked at the clock it was only half eleven. It just feels like this day has been going on forever. Anyway, the stupid book is now sitting on my head. I have read the blurb and it looks awful. Apparently it is about a girl called Ruthie (oh my God, my mother is pathologically obsessed with the letter 'r' – she can't even call a fictional child by a name starting with another letter. What does it mean? A psychologist would have a field day with her). Anyway, Ruthie really wants a boyfriend and comes up with all sorts of schemes to meet a boy. And then she meets one on holiday. Yawn. I'm going to start reading it now.

LATER

Oh my God. I have read nearly the entire book and unless it improves dramatically in the last thirty pages I am never talking to my mother again. Well, actually, I'm not talking to her again anyway. But still. Ruthie is horrible. She and her equally horrible friends are obsessed with boys. Now despite what Rachel may say about my pure and holy love for Paperboy, I am not obsessed with boys. I may be slightly obsessed with Paperboy, and a few very good-looking guitarists, and a couple of actors, but I'm not obsessed with boys in general. But Ruthie just thinks about boys and nothing else. She doesn't, like, read anything, or listen to music apart from boy bands. She would never take part in a spontaneous synchronised dance session. Also, she and her friends are really annoying. They say things like 'you go, girl!' and are really sassy. Sassy people are always obnoxious in real life. Ruthie and her friends never laugh about anything. They just give each other makeovers and go shopping. Where do they get the money to go shopping? It's not like Mum hands over loads of cash to me. Far from it, in fact.

Anyway. Basically the book is all about how Ruthie and her friends have a competition to see who will get a boyfriend first. Also, they are in a girl band together and sing drippy songs into their hairbrushes. They do all sorts of stupid sad things like pretending to like football so random boys will like them. And at one stage Ruthie follows a boy into a toilet! That sounds kind of filthy but THANK GOD there are no sexy goings-on in the book. I'd have to emigrate if there were. Anyway, they are all really competitive and their crappy girl band breaks up because they play lots of tricks on each other and I actually can't understand why they're friends at all as they all secretly seem to hate each other. In the end they all go and eat pizza together and realise the virtues of friendship and how it's more important than boys, but frankly if I had managed to escape from the society of these horrible cows for five minutes it would take a lot more than a pizza to make me see any of them ever again.

LATER

Just after I wrote that last line there was a knock on the door. I shouted, 'Go away!', but it turned out to be Rachel so I let her in. We are no longer enemies. We are fellow sufferers. Rachel has also read the book. She is almost angrier than me, which I didn't believe was possible, but she really really is because there is something in the book which actually did happen to her. She won't tell me what it is, but she says it is pretty tragic (of course, she said that this mysterious INCIDENT took place when she was 'your age', as if girls my age are automatically stupider than sixteen-year-olds, which is obviously rubbish, as one look at Rachel and her friends will prove). Anyway, she also said that she never told Mum about it, but she did, of course, tell Jenny about it on the phone, and as there is sadly no privacy in our house Mum must have overheard her. She says there's no chance that this is a coincidence because of 'certain details' (I have to admit that this all makes this book a lot more interesting – I must figure out what this story is).

'So not only is she embarrassing us, she's SPYING on us. Or she was in the past,' said Rachel. The last time I saw her so angry was when Bumpers did a poo in Tom's bag when he was in our house (Tom, of course, not Bumpers, who is always here). 'And the worst thing is that this ... incident doesn't just involve me, it was Jenny as well. So she's going to think I've been telling Mum about stuff and she'll kill me.'

'Surely she won't,' I said. 'She'll understand that our mother is an evil spy.'

'Yeah, well, I hope so,' said Rachel. 'I'm going round to her house now to warn her in advance. What are you doing?'

I told her I was planning on hiding myself away and that I needed something good to read to remind myself that all literature is not totally evil and life-destroying, but I didn't know what I was in the mood for.

'I know,' said Rachel, and she went to her room and

came back with a copy of *Pride and Prejudice*. 'There you go,' she said, 'read that.'

I told her I didn't know if I was in the mood for something old-fashioned right now, but she said, 'Trust me, Bex. The heroine has a very, very embarrassing mother. Jane Austen understands our pain.'

LATER

Oh my God, Jane Austen DOES understand my pain! Well, the pain of having a mother you kind of want to shoot, anyway. At least Mum isn't trying to marry off me and Rachel. Unless that's what happens in the next Ruthie book. *Pride and Prejudice* is about a girl called Lizzie with lots of sisters whose mother wants them all to get married and embarrasses them every time they leave the house, especially in front of Mr Darcy, who is this annoying rude but hunky man who's just turned up in the neighbourhood.

LATER

I am imagining Mr Darcy looking a bit like Paperboy.

LATER

Although I can't imagine Paperboy on a horse. But who knows what he gets up to when he's not delivering papers? He could be quite the horseman for all I know.

LATER

Finally got through to Cass, but I wish I hadn't now. Some friend she is. I told her about what Rachel said about Mum putting something from her own life in it. Cass seemed more worried that there'll be something about *her* in the book rather than about *my* public humiliation. She was so annoying I told her that there's a bit in the book about that time she took off her glasses when we were in Tower Records so she'd look better in front of a very cute boy who was looking at some music magazines. She was posing away by the magazine racks until she realised she was staring straight at the porn section. I let her rave on for a while before I told her it wasn't true (although I will have to be careful what I say on the phone from now on as apparently the walls have ears in this house of spies. Well, one spy. Unless she's got Dad doing her dirty work and reporting to her on our conversations. You never know). Anyway, she calmed down a bit then and was a bit more sympathetic. For about five seconds. She said the photo of me in the paper was nice.

'Your hair looks very shiny,' she said.

'That's because I stole Mum's conditioner,' I said.

Cass said, 'So she's good for something, then.'

'Yeah, I suppose so,' I said. 'But anyway, I'm making a stupid face in the photo.'

And then Cass who, lest we forget, is meant to be comforting me in my hour of sorrow, said, 'But you always look a little bit funny in photos.'

And she is supposedly my friend! She says she meant it as a compliment because I look much better (or as she kindly puts it 'quite normal') in real life. But it is not what I want to hear right now when that hideous photo is in newspapers all over the country. So I said, 'Well, thanks a million' and hung up. She texted back straight away and begged for my forgiveness (as well she might) so I texted her and said she was forgiven and I suppose she is, but I'm still very annoyed with her.

LATER

I rang Alice, who was much more understanding than selfish Cass. I feel a bit better now I've talked to her. She said that no one at school will care that much about the book, and no one reads the paper anyway. She said I am worrying about something that MIGHT happen rather than something that has already happened. She sounded so wise that for a while I actually forgot all about the hideously embarrassing Paperboy incident from this morning, which definitely did happen. But still. I don't feel quite as bad as I did earlier. I am going to have to leave my room now. I want to have a shower and I'm starving again. But I'm still not talking to my horrible evil mother.

SUNDAY

I am still not talking to Mum. Neither is Rachel. Well, we kind of grunt when spoken to, but that's about it. I made my own dinner last night (scrambled eggs and sossies, which I suppose is quite a lot of eggs in one day. Unfortunately it turns out that everything nice I can cook is somehow egg-related) and took it up to eat in my room. Rachel just went off to Jenny's house. Dad gave us a lecture this afternoon about acting like babies but he doesn't understand our shame. I feel sick to my stomach whenever I think of Paperboy seeing that photo of me. And seeing me looking like a lunatic in my pyjamas. Oh, the whole thing is too awful to think about. I'm going to go to bed, to read more *Pride and Prejudice.*

MONDAY

I was going to write 'today was the worst day of my life',

but the way things are going around here at the moment I'll end up writing that every day, so I'll just say that today was as terrible as I thought it would be and it's all my mother's fault. As usual. At first I thought that it was actually going to be quite a good day: first of all, I was a bit late but not too late – I arrived just as the second bell was going so I was able to sneak into the classroom with Alice and Cass and not talk to anyone. Then we had English first class (which I had been totally dreading, for obvious reasons) and it turned out that Mrs Harrington wasn't in so we all had to go the library. We always pray that we'll have a free class, but our teachers are apparently immune to all germs as they are hardly ever out sick. Us girls will be wheezing and coughing and puking away and not a single germ do those teachers catch. So anyway, we had a free class, and I thought I could just sit there and read something entertaining, but Karen Rodgers was sitting behind me. I don't know if I've mentioned Karen Rodgers before. One day during the summer Cass and Alice and I were in a strangely hippyish mood, talking about how cool it is that our class actually all get on pretty well with each other and how there's a genuinely friendly atmosphere, and then

Cass remembered Karen Rodgers and Alice and I both went 'oh, yeah' in exactly the same depressed tone. Karen Rodgers isn't a bully, but it's not for want of trying. She's just kind of mean and sarky and she's always making un-funny jokes at other people's expense. Her best (and only) friend is Alison Smith, who is actually okay, if a bit annoying, when she's on her own, but when Karen is around she turns into a sniggering sidekick.

So anyway. No sooner had I taken *Pride and Prejudice* out of my bag than something poked me in the back. I turned around and Karen was smirking at me and waving a pencil.

'What?' I said, in my rudest voice. Well, rudest whisper.

'I saw you in the paper,' said Karen. 'Were you making that face on purpose?'

I felt myself go red with rage, but I couldn't think of anything clever to say so I just turned around and ignored Karen's hideous sniggering (I should have said, 'Yeah, I was doing an impersonation of you.' Damn. I just thought of that now. Why didn't I think of that this morning?). She poked me in the back again. but luckily Miss Brady, the school librarian, noticed and told her to stop. Miss Brady is a bit scary so Karen did stop and as soon as the free class was over I marched out before she could poke me again with her revolting pencil. It really is disgusting. She chews the end so it's all gross and falling to bits. Why is she eating wood anyway? Perhaps she is part beaver.

But worse was to come. When the free class was over we were walking to the next class and on the way a few girls from other years pointed at me and whispered to each other. I heard a senior girl going 'yeah, she was in the paper at the weekend. Her mum wrote a book about her or something!' And then things got even worse. The next class was in Room 7, which is our class 2:2's form room (which means we have lunch there and our lockers are there) and when we went in, we saw that someone had got the awful photo of me and Mum and put it up on the noticeboard. And they'd blown it up on a photocopier so it was huge. That was all bad enough. But someone had written '2:2's OWN PAGE THREE GIRL' above the photo. Everyone stared at the photo and then at me and lots of them were laughing. I wanted to die. But then, without saying a word, Alice marched straight over, tore it down, crumpled it up, and without missing a beat she threw it all the way across the room into the bin. A perfect shot! Who knew she had such good aim? She should join the second-year basketball team. Everyone was so surprised by this that they shut up and then our maths teacher Miss Condren came in so that was the end of that. But the feeling that everyone was laughing at me behind my back went on all day. Alice and Cass said I'm just being paranoid but I know I'm not.

In fact, the world seems to have gone mad. Vanessa Finn was nice to me at lunch today. It was very weird. She usually just ignores me, which is fine by me. In fact she ignores almost all of us because she thinks we're common. But not today. Me and Cass and Alice and Ellie and Emma Donnelly were lurking in the cloakroom and they were all being very kind and telling me that everything will blow over, and I was actually feeling okay as long as I could hide there forever. But I had to go to the loo (I shouldn't have drunk that smoothie so quickly) and on the way back Vanessa just leaped out in front of me (well, she didn't quite leap, she just walked round a corner, but it felt like being leaped out on) and said, 'Hi, Rebecca!' in a strangely friendly voice.

'Hi,' I said, and tried to walk past her, but she moved in front of me (she is surprisingly nimble for someone who spends most of her time wearing ginormous fluffy boots).

'So, how are you?' she said.

'Grand,' I said. 'Sorry, I'm just ...'

'I just wanted to say that I thought that photo of you in the paper was so cool,' she said.

'What?!' I said.

'Yeah, you looked great,' she said.

'Um, thanks,' I said. And then the bell rang for class, so I sort of smiled and went back to the others to get my bag. I have to admit, I was genuinely touched. Maybe she is not such a snooty cow after all? She is obviously not telling the truth, as I did not look great in that photo, but it is quite kind of her to lie to me. Although she is still a bit odd.

Anyway, the afternoon went past in a sort of blur apart from the bits between classes where it felt like everyone was staring at me until (AT LAST) the final bell rang. I went back to my locker to dump some stuff while Cass and Alice got their blazers and Karen bloody Rodgers was there. She was smirking at me (it seems to be her default expression) and when I was leaving she said, 'Watch out for the paparazzi!' And her horrible sidekick Alison laughed like this was the funniest thing anyone has ever said in the history of the world. I hate both of them.

At least I'm home now. You can take it for granted, by the way, that I'm still not talking to Mum, but I had to give in and eat her food. I couldn't take any more eggs. Or sausages. So I grudgingly shovelled in some lentil and chicken casserole this evening. Lentils sound disgusting but actually they are delicious when they're mixed up with chicken and bacon and mushrooms and stuff, and that casserole is one of my favourite things – I think Mum might be trying to win me round with food. I can't be bought that easily, though. Not after a day like today. When will this nightmare end?!

TUESDAY

What is up with Vanessa Finn? She was being weird again today. I was getting stuff out of my locker this morning and when I closed the door she was standing behind it smiling. I would have shrieked if I hadn't given up shrieking forever after the Paperboy incident.

'So!' she said. 'How are you?'

'Um ... okay,' I said. 'Fine.' Her sudden friendliness is making me nervous.

'How are you finding being a celebrity?' She was still smiling in a slightly mad way.

'I'm not,' I said. 'A celebrity, I mean.'

'Oh, come on, you're like, completely famous now,' she said.

'Well, not really,' I said. 'I mean, it was just one ...' But Vanessa interrupted me.

'You were in two papers,' she said.

'I didn't know you paid so much attention to papers,' I said, trying to edge around her.

'Of course I don't,' said Vanessa (sounding like more like her usual snooty self). 'My mum was reading it and I saw the photo of you and said, 'God, that's that girl from my class at school'. And my mum was, like, so impressed and said that your mum is some super-famous celebrity writer, or something. My mum's, like, obsessed with your mum's books.'

Oh God, not another one.

'Oh,' I said.

'So yeah,' said Vanessa, 'I didn't know your mum was a famous writer, or whatever.' Well, at least someone hasn't been paying any attention to Mrs Harrington all term. That's kind of good to know. 'You don't have the same surname, do you?'

'No,' I said. 'Rafferty's my dad's surname. My mum didn't change her name when she got married.' I'd done it! I'd squeezed around her. 'Um, I'll see you later, Vanessa.' And I ran out of the room down the corridor before she could say anything else. But why is she being so weirdly friendly to me in the first place? I don't think it's really kindness. She's up to something. Although maybe she has just taken a good look at the state of my hair and realised that at least one of her classmates is definitely not going to be a hairdresser. Anyway, it is starting to get annoying.

And it was not the only annoying part of today. Karen Rodgers, whose life is apparently so boring she has to look to me for entertainment, had great fun with her stupid little pal at lunch today talking very loudly about SOME PEOPLE who supposedly think they're SO COOL because their MOTHER wrote a BOOK about them.

This is particularly irritating because of course I don't think it's cool my mother wrote a book that possibly has some connection to me (I refuse to acknowledge that Ruthie O'Reilly's life could actually be mine). I hope that everyone in the class remembers this and that Karen doesn't brainwash them into thinking I love it.

However, today was not all bad. Mrs Harrington is still sick. Maybe she'll die? At least that would solve one problem.

LATER

I feel a bit guilty about wishing Mrs Harrington would die. I didn't mean it really. Obviously. But what if she does? Die, I mean. I'll have cursed her!

I am sort of talking to Mum. She asked me whether I would prefer roast chicken or spaghetti carbonara for dinner tomorrow. I had to answer. After all, we don't get to have roast chicken that often. Who knew food was my weak spot? I can only cook eggs! I'm hardly a gourmet.

WEDNESDAY ✿

Mrs Harrington still not in. I can't pretend I'm not glad, but I'm starting to get a bit worried about the whole possibly-cursing-her thing. I'm also getting a bit worried about Vanessa. She was being all friendly again today. She asked me if I wanted to go out to her house after school and look at her designs for her giant birthday party (yes, designs. She is designing decorations for some sort of giant tent marquee thing). I didn't, obviously, and it was a completely weird thing to ask someone you've barely spoken to for a year, but I was polite and said I had to go straight home. I would like to think that she has just realised how wonderful I am after sharing a class with me for a year, but I'm afraid that's probably not true. What is she up to?

But anyway, I don't care about her so much at the moment, because this evening when we were eating our dinner (roast chicken, yum yum) Rachel said something that has given me a brilliant idea.

'Hey,' she said, pouring nearly all the gravy on to her

plate before I'd even got near the gravy jug. 'Tom's friend Sam is moving to America for a year and he has to find someone to look after his drum kit. I'm sure you lot won't know anyone who could take it in, but I said I'd ask.'

That's when I had my idea.

'I'll take it,' I said.

'No you won't,' said Mum. 'I'm not having noisy drums in this house.'

'Ha!' said Rachel. 'Like you could play the drums.'

'First of all, for our information,' I said haughtily, 'I have always wanted to play the drums. Well, sort of. I like tapping along to music on my desk with pencils.'

'Yeah, I know, and it's really annoying,' said Rachel.

'No it's not. Anyway, I think I'd be able to play the drums really well. And second of all, I'd keep them at Alice's house. They've got a million big stables and barns and stuff out there. Well, they've got those stables next to the house, and that garage, and the barn at the other side of the yard. And there's nothing in any of them except a few old lawnmowers and rakes and things. Me and Alice used to joke about starting a band and using one as our rehearsal room. And now we can actually do it!'

Mum looked at me. She's trying to be nice since she wrecked my life with her stupid book. 'Well, if Alice's parents don't mind, maybe that's a good idea.'

'It's a ridiculous idea!' said Rachel. 'You can't just sit there playing drums on your own! You don't have a band!'

'I'll start one,' I said. Well, why shouldn't I? Alice can play the classical guitar, after all, and Cass, well, Cass can play the piano. She's been having lessons for years, she's on grade 4 or something. Guitar, keyboard and drums are enough to start a band. We wouldn't have a bass player but they're not that important anyway. And we can all sing. Well, sort of. Well, Alice can. Although do I want Alice to be, like, the frontwoman and band leader? I kind of want to do that myself. But I can't sing and play drums at the same time, can I? Anyway, we can sort all that out later. After dinner I rushed straight up to my room to phone Alice and told her my idea. I thought she'd be a bit hard to persuade, especially as I was suggesting we take over her place as our practising room, but she was actually really enthusiastic.

'I've always wanted to start a band!' she said. 'And we can use my dad's old electric guitar! Well, we can use it once I get an amp.'

'I know, we should have done this ages ago,' I said.

'Well, you didn't have the drums,' said Alice.

'Oh, yeah,' I said. 'Well, I have them now! Or I will soon. Rachel rang Tom and he rang Sam and I can get the drums on Saturday! Mum said she'll take me to get them and then we can go straight out to your house if it's okay with your mum and dad.'

'They'll love it,' said Alice. 'They'll probably want to join in. Don't worry, I won't let them.' We talked about where exactly we would have our practice room. I thought the barn would be quite cool, because we could pretend it was a big music venue, but Alice said, 'We can put the drums in the garage, because it's the only one of those old buildings with electricity.'

I hadn't even thought of that. Alice's sensibleness is very useful. It probably comes from living in the countryside. She is full of practical rural wisdom. And of course if she was still living around here, she wouldn't have all those barns and things.

'That garage is very basic, you know,' she said. 'If all those buildings had been, like, done up, we'd never have been able to afford the house. Remember what the house was like when we moved in?'

I did, it practically had no walls. They'd had to live in two rooms for about six months. Luckily it was in summer so it was quite fun (well, we were only eleven at the time) and I used to come out here and stay over – it was like camping.

'I'm not expecting a luxurious studio!' I said. That will come later, of course. When we're famous, as we inevitably will be.

After talking to Alice, I rang Cass, but to my amazement she wasn't quite as excited.

'I can't exactly take our piano out there,' she said.

'You can use Alice's mum's keyboard!' Alice's mum decided a few years ago that she wanted to learn the piano and got a keyboard instead. It's quite big but not as big as a piano and we can get it out to the garage pretty easily. Anyway, that wasn't enough for Princess Cass.

'I can't play indie music,' she said. 'I can only play, like, Mozart and Debussy. Not the sort of stuff we'd want to play in our band.'

'Oh, don't be silly, Cass,' I said. 'You won't have to play

big keyboard solos. You can use the cool electric sound on your keyboard and play bass lines and things.'

'Oh,' said Cass. She didn't say anything for a few moments.

'What are you doing?' I said. I wasn't used to her being so silent.

'I'm thinking,' said Cass.

'Oh,' I said.

Then Cass sighed and said, 'Oh, okay, I'll do it. As long as you don't expect me to be particularly good.'

'Hurray!'

'But don't get too excited,' she said. I promised her I wouldn't. But I am excited! I'm excited about the whole thing, and it seems like ages since I was excited about anything. Mum's horrible book doesn't count, because that didn't make me excited in a good way; it just made me angry. But the band will be loads of fun. We can write songs and play gigs and make t-shirts and it will be brilliant. And it will be the sort of thing stupid Ruthie O'Reilly would hate. Ha!

THURSDAY ☾

Mrs Harrington was back today. I no longer feel guilty for possibly cursing her. She had the flu, and as she told the entire class, it wasn't so bad 'because I was able to read Rebecca's mammy's new book!'

Everyone, even my own friends, turned around and stared at me. Some of them, like Alice and Cass and Ellie, were looking at me with sympathy and pity. Others, and I think you can guess who, were sniggering away like stupid pencil-eating fools.

'And it was brilliant, of course!' said Mrs Harrington. 'Now I know all about what you and your friends get up to, Rebecca!'

As soon as she said that, my friends stopped looking sympathetic and started looking appalled. Ha! Now they know how I feel.

'Well,' I said. 'I mean. It's not like it's actually about us. I'm nothing like Ruthie whatserface.'

'She's really not,' said Cass.

Mrs Harrington laughed like this was the funniest thing in the world. 'You can't fool me, girls! I read that report in the paper where Rebecca's mammy said she based it on her and her sister's antics. I'm not going to ask who won the competition, though!'

I thought I was going to get sick. And then, as if this wasn't bad enough, Karen Rodgers said, 'What competition?'

Now, my friends haven't read the evil book yet, but they know what it's about because I told them just how awful it was. So when Karen Rodgers said this, Alice and Cass and Ellie and Emma all stared at Mrs Harrington like they were trying to hypnotise her into shutting up.

It didn't work, of course.

'Haven't you read it yet?' said Mrs Harrington in a surprised voice, like she couldn't understand why everyone in the world wasn't queuing up to read Mum's stupid books. 'It's great fun. It's all about girls who have a competition to see who will get a boyfriend first – not a good idea, girls!'

Of course, everyone in the class started laughing, not just Karen Bitchface Rodgers. 'But Ruth and her friends learn a valuable lesson in the book – and what's that, Rebecca?'

'What?' I said. 'Um, I don't know. How to be complete idiots who are always horrible to each other?'

Mrs Harrington laughed as though this were a joke. 'Oh, I can see you've inherited your mother's wicked sense of humour! No, the girls learn that the most important thing is friendship. And that nothing is worth losing your friends over, not even a perfect boyfriend. Isn't that right, Rebecca?'

'I suppose so,' I said nervously.

'So I know all you girls are going to enjoy this book,' Harrington went on. For a dreadful moment I thought she was going to announce that we were going to be studying it in class instead of *Great Expectations*. I wouldn't put it past her. But she just said, 'It certainly made having the flu more entertaining!' and then actually started talking about ordinary English class things.

After class, of course, everyone found it hilarious to talk about the book. It wasn't like they were being mean about it (apart from Karen, of course), but it was very annoying.

'You didn't really have a competition, did you?' said Jessie McCabe.

'Of course we didn't!' said Cass.

'She's just saying that because in real life none of them actually won,' said Karen Rodgers. 'I haven't seen them with any gorgeous boyfriends, have you?'

'I haven't seen you with one either,' said Cass. 'You're obviously too busy spying on us.'

Karen snorted through her nose at this like a baby pig, but she went off with Alison. Alison looked back at us slightly apologetically. I bet she's a bit embarrassed by Karen's rudeness sometimes. She's not that bad, really. But I'd like her a bit more if she ever actually stood up to her so-called best friend.

Luckily, there are more exciting things in my life to distract me from all this rubbish. We spent all of lunchtime talking about the band. We haven't come up with a good name yet. The good thing is that Cass is much more enthusiastic about it now.

'You just put me on the spot,' she said. 'I don't want you two relying on me to be really good, because I mightn't be. But I'll give it a shot.'

'I bet you're much better than you think you are,' said Alice. 'I mean, Rebecca's never even played the drums at all, so you're bound to be better than her. No offence, Bex.'

'I've played the pencils,' I said. 'I know how to keep a beat.'

'You are quite good at the pencils,' said Cass.

This evening I got two wooden spoons and tried playing the drums on the sofa cushions. It was pretty easy, really. I was playing along to the songs on Phantom FM when Rachel came in and burst out laughing.

'What do you think you're doing?' she said. 'You do realize that playing the drums isn't the same as playing a … a couch, don't you?' And she started laughing again.

'It won't be that much different,' I said.

'Yes it will! You've got to use your feet!'

'What? No I don't!'

'Of course you do! How do you think they play that big bass drum? The big drum facing the audience, with the band logo on it? You have to play it with a foot pedal. Oh my God, I can't wait to see you try the real thing, it'll be hilarious.' And she went off, sniggering. She's so superior and annoying.

LATER

She does have a point, though. I didn't know about the feet thing. Perhaps playing the drums is harder than it looks.

LATER

Oh, it can't be though, look at some of the people who do it.

FRIDAY ✡

I had an actual conversation with Paperboy! Well, sort of. He looked particularly good this evening. I think he gets better every time I see him. I ran out to answer the door when the bell rang but unfortunately just as I reached the hall I tripped over the straps of Rachel's stupid bag which of course she had left in the middle of the floor. She is so careless. But I had regained my composure by the time I opened the door. I think. I have a horrible feeling my hair was all over the place. Anyway, Paperboy sort of smiled and said, 'So, you weren't in the paper again this week. I thought this was going to be a regular thing.' I tried to think of something really funny and smart to say so he would go away thinking what a witty, attractive girl I was but all I could think of was 'um, no, my mum decided to stop embarrassing me for a while.' And he laughed and said, 'Good for you,' and then he asked for the paper money and I gave it to him and he said, 'Cheers, see you' and went off, and, to be honest, I was quite relieved because, although of course it is brilliant actually having a conversation with Paperboy, it is also a bit stressful.

Drums tomorrow!

SATURDAY ★

I HAVE DRUMS!

Well, not in my actual possession. They're in Alice's garage. But they're mine (for the moment) and I played them and I hate to admit it, but Rachel was right and they are a bit harder than the cushions. But I wasn't that bad (even Sam said so, so HA! to Rachel).

Mum and Rachel (she had to come because she knows Sam) and I all went out to Sam's house at about ten o'clock. Sam was really nice. He is one of Tom's best friends. The drums were in the dining room and he had left them up so he could tell me what each drum was called and give me a quick lesson while Mum and Rachel had a cup of tea with his parents in the kitchen. So I had my first drumming session, and it was actually pretty hard – I could play a beat for a couple of minutes but then I'd get a bit confused about which of the drums I was meant to be hitting. And the cymbals were quite tricky too. Working the pedal was the hardest, though – every time I concentrated on getting the pedal beat right, I'd forget what I was meant to be doing with my hands.

But Sam said I'd get the hang of it soon enough. Then he showed me how to take the drum kit apart (you've got to unscrew lots of weird little keys and things) and put it back together again (I'm glad he did that because I wouldn't have been able to do it properly on my own). He even did a little diagram for me! He is quite good looking too (although not as good looking as Paperboy). I asked him if he was looking forward to going to America and he said not really because he'll have to come back next year and do sixth year again (well, sort of again, he's just started sixth year now), but he's looking forward to seeing New York (his mum's job has something to do with the U.N.). And when I told him about my plans to start a band with Cass and Alice and about how Alice had an electric guitar but no amp he lent me a little amp and some microphones and their stands as well. 'Someone might as well put them to good use,' he said. He is brilliant. I sort of wish he wasn't going to America at all. I would like to see him again. Even though he is (a) too old and (b) my heart belongs to Paperboy.

Anyway! We got the drum kit and the amp and the microphones and stuff into the car and took it out to Alice's. Mum went off to chat to Alice's parents, who were all excited about her stupid new book. They both love Mum's books, God help them. Alice says Germans love sloppy books about Ireland, and that's why her mum first came over here in the eighties, because she'd read loads about the beauty of the countryside and how friendly and magical the people supposedly were. That is why she loves Mum's books so much. Although Alice's dad is from

Clontarf, so he doesn't have any excuse. Anyway, I put the kit back together again (the diagram helped, and so did Alice and even Rachel). And then there it was. Our band room (well, band garage). Alice's guitar was there already, and it was propped up against the bass drum and it really looked like a proper band rehearsal room.

'Except you can't play the drums and you don't have any songs,' said Rachel. She is so annoying. She and Mum went home (Mum came back later to collect me – she is still feeling guilty about destroying my life so she is being very good about lifts) and Alice and I sort of looked at the drums and then at each other and then we got very excited and jumped up and down and cheered.

'Let's play something!' said Alice, and I said she should start playing something and I'd try playing along. Alice has been learning classical guitar but of course she can play chords and stuff too, so she plugged in her dad's guitar. But we couldn't start rocking straight away because she had to tune it first which took about five years. Then she did a big chord. Even though the amp is tiny it sounded pretty good. It sounded very rock and roll.

'Wow,' said Alice. And we both looked at each other

and started laughing. Then she started playing a song by that sixties band the Kinks – the one that goes 'all day and all of the night'. It only has three chords in it so she could just about manage it. I started drumming along and it was a bit wonky and I couldn't work out the foot pedal thing but it worked! Well, I was more or less in time with the music. I am a drummer! We tried a few more songs and Alice sang a bit (she says it's hard to play and sing at the same time but she did quite well) and I was surprised at how tiring it was, bashing away. But it was brilliant. It was the most fun I've had in ages and ages. We're going to have another practice tomorrow – Cass is coming out too.

SUNDAY

First proper band practice today! It went really well, to my surprise. I say surprise, because the way Cass was going on I thought we'd have to spend the entire time helping her turn on the keyboard. She was acting like she barely knew how to play the piano even though she's done her grade 4 exams, which apparently means she should be able to play fairly complicated stuff. When we got off the bus at the end of Alice's road (or rather, country lane, because it's not really what you'd call a road. There's grass growing in the middle of it and only two other houses apart from theirs. Also, it's about 20 metres long) she was still moaning on about how crap she was going to be which was weird because Cass is hardly ever nervous. On the worrying scale, Alice is probably the most neurotic, then me, and then, a long way away, Cass. But today she was all over the place. It was very surprising. However, when she saw the practice room (as we are now calling the garage) she cheered up a bit.

'Wow,' she said. 'It does look very ... official.'

'Will we try that Kinks' song?' said Alice. Cass thought she didn't know it and started dithering again but then she realised she did know it after all and we got going. And it sounded ... well, not good, exactly, but it sounded like music. Cass realised that playing bass lines on the keyboards is actually pretty easy if you have any sense of rhythm at all (which she does, thank God) and she figured one out pretty quickly. In fact, I hate to say it, but I think I myself might be the weakest link at the moment. I can't quite get the hang of the cymbals yet. Or the whole playing-the-bass-drum-with-my-feet thing. I wish I could take the drums home so I could practise during the week but that's not very practical. I'd never get them on the bus, for one. And there's no way Mum would help me lug them around the place. Anyway, I can practise playing the drums on cushions, even though Rachel tells me to stop every time I start, because apparently the faint noise of drumsticks hitting cushions 'drives her mad'. She should count herself lucky I can't take the drums home, you can barely hear those cushions.

Anyway, we are all very excited about the band. But we're not going to tell anybody about it. It was Cass's idea, and she's probably right.

'They might want to hear us. Or they'll want to know the names of songs and stuff,' she said. 'And we won't have anything to tell them so we'll look mad. We should wait until we can actually, you know, play more than one song.'

I think this might be a good idea.

MONDAY

Ugh. I hate my school. I spent the entire day wishing I was practising my lovely drums instead of sitting in that stupid place. Apparently my mother doesn't even bother telling me when she's going to humiliate me now. It seems there was an article yesterday in some newspaper we don't get at home all about Mum and her stupid new book. And as well as a ginormous picture of Mum (which, sadly, is the sort of thing I'm used to by now), there were photos of me and Rachel as small kids! Dancing around on a beach in stupid pink shorts! I remember that photo being taken – it was when we were on holiday in Kerry when we were little. We were working out a dance routine to a Destiny's Child song. One of these photos was on the noticeboard in our classroom when I got into school today.

No prizes for guessing who was sniggering away next to it.

'Hey, Rafferty,' said Karen. 'I see you were in the paper again. Looking good!'

'Oh, thanks,' I said. 'I'll lend you my lovely shorts if you like.'

And I just sat down at my desk. Luckily that was when Miss Kelly came in and started talking about polar bears dying horribly. I've never been so glad to be terrified. After the class Ellie pulled down the picture and tore it up. Thank God she did, because our next class was in the same room and it was Mrs Harrington. Imagine if she'd been going on about those shorts! She was awful as it was. We are meant to be doing *Romeo and Juliet*, but Mrs Harrington keeps going on about the importance of romantic love. The thought of her getting romantic with anyone is too much.

Then after the class was over, Vanessa Finn proved she really has lost her mind by saying 'Hey, Rebecca, I thought you looked really cool in that photo' as she passed by me and Cass. She is definitely insane. There is no way on earth she can possibly think that is true.

Anyway, at lunchtime I went to find Rachel to warn her about Mum's latest betrayal. I never usually look for her at school, as we generally pretend we don't know each other while on school grounds, but recent events have made us realise we need to stick together. I stuck my head in the door of her form room and one of her classmates said, 'Oh God, Rache, is that your sister? I didn't recognise her without her lovely shorts.'

So obviously Rachel already knew about the disaster. But she came out to me anyway. She was all red and cross-looking.

'What is it?' she said snappishly.

'Oh, charming,' I said. 'I came over here to warn you about that stupid article and this is the thanks I get.'

Rachel looked slightly ashamed of herself, for once.

'Sorry,' she said. 'Oh God, I can't believe she gave them that photo.'

'Rafferty!' came a voice from inside Rachel's classroom. 'Are you and Rebecca practising your dance routine again?' It was her friend Jenny, so I knew she was only joking, but Rachel looked like she was going to explode.

'This,' she said, 'is the final straw.'

'We hope it is,' I said. 'Who knows what Mum has planned next?'

Who indeed? When I got home I politely asked Mum about that terrible article.

'Where did they get that horrible, horrible photo of me and Rachel?' I bellowed.

Mum looked uncomfortable.

'I gave it to them, of course. And before you start shouting and roaring, it was a few weeks ago, before I realised how upset you'd be about the whole thing. I thought you'd think it was funny.'

'FUNNY?' I shrieked. Then Rachel came in and started shouting too. Eventually Mum stopped looking apologetic and started looking cross.

'Look girls,' she said. 'I have to give interviews to promote the book. I do this for all my books. It's part of my job, which is selling books, so that your dad and I can pay the mortgage and look after you two. We need this money and this is part of how I earn it. So unless you'd like to have no new clothes or nice holidays in France or dancing classes ...'

'We haven't gone to dancing classes since I was ten,' said Rachel grumpily.

'Oh for God's sake! Well, no pocket money or new shoes or iPods or new music. That is what my job and your dad's job pays for, as well as the food on the table and the clothes on your backs and the roof over your head, and it would be nice if you ever appreciated it!' And she looked very cross and walked out of the room.

Rachel and I looked at each other.

'She has a point,' said Rachel.

'Well, she would if she hadn't given them that photo. I mean, no one made her do it,' I said.

'True,' said Rachel. We tried not to speak to Mum for the rest of the evening, but I don't think she even noticed. Some mother she is.

Dad is, of course, on her side. 'I know it was embarrassing,' he said. 'But your mother really did think you'd find it funny. So did I. I mean, it's a lovely photo of the two of you.'

'It might be lovely in a family photo album,' said Rachel. 'Although that's a matter of opinion. It's not lovely in a newspaper that somehow everyone in school managed to see. I don't even know how they did it. It's not like that paper puts every article online.'

'Well, if it's any consolation, all this publicity stuff will be over soon,' said Dad. 'And then everyone will forget about it.'

He seemed very confident about this, but I bet they won't. I'm going to get compared to that awful Ruthie O'Reilly for the rest of my life. I know I will.

TUESDAY

We can't decide what to call the band. We spent most of lunchtime hiding under the coats in the cloakroom having a discussion about it. I think some of the others wondered what on earth we were being so secretive about. Anyway, we all had lots of ideas but none of them seemed quite right.

'Should it be a "The" name?' said Cass. 'You know, like The Beatles.'

'The Girls with Evil Mothers,' I said.

'My mother's okay,' said Alice.

'Mine's about a medium,' said Cass. 'Not perfect but not totally evil either. So no.'

'Okay, okay,' I said. 'I didn't mean it really. Ummm ... the Does.'

'The what?' said Cass.

'The Does,' I said. 'Like the dear. Doe, a dear, a female deer ...'

'We'd have to explain it to everyone,' said Alice. 'Otherwise they'd think it was d'oh, like Homer Simpson.'

'Oh yeah, good point,' I said.

'Maybe it should be a Someone and the Somethings name,' said Alice. 'Like Florence and the Machine.'

'But then whose name would we use?' I said. 'You, me or Cass?'

'Alice and the ... Antidotes,' said Alice, dreamily.

'We're not your backing band, Alice,' said Cass.

'And all of us sing anyway,' I said.

'Okay, okay,' said Alice. 'It was only an idea.'

We lay on the ground of the cloakroom and thought. We came up with a few more names (Daisychain, Kitten Attack, The Antidote), but they just weren't very good. None of them seemed right. I never realised finding the right band name could be so difficult.

'We'll know the right one when we see it,' said sage-like Alice.

'But what if we don't see it?' said Cass. 'We've got to pick a name at some stage. Imagine if you had a baby and let it go this long without a name. Everyone would say it was child abuse.'

'I'm not sure our band is quite as important as a baby,' said Alice.

She's probably right. I suppose. It's quite important to us, though. So we really have to come up with a name.

WEDNESDAY ✿

Well, we've come up with a name now, but I wish we hadn't. Not because of the name, but how it happened.

Today was awful. First of all, everyone in the class knows about the band now. We didn't really plan on telling anyone until we were actually, you know, able to play properly, but I couldn't help it. It happened at lunchtime. We'd just sat through Mrs O'Reilly blathering on about Christopher Columbus and his ridiculously-named ships for forty-five minutes and another Miss Kelly geography class (she spent about twenty minutes telling us about what we'll have to do to survive once all the water runs out. I will have nightmares for weeks). This was all traumatic enough, and I was not in the mood for Karen Rodgers and her nonsense. But Karen has somehow managed to get her paws on Mum's book AND she's read it. I can't believe she got through it so quickly. I didn't even know she could read.

Anyway, I knew someone would read the book eventually, and I knew it would probably be someone like Karen who doesn't like me, but it didn't make it any more fun. We had a free class in the library and when we arrived the librarian wasn't there and there were no teachers around. Alice and I were having a look at the fiction shelves when Karen suddenly produced a copy of *May the Best Girl Win* from God knows where (probably her pants).

'Hey, everyone!' she cried. 'Look what I've got!'

And of course everyone laughed. Not Cass or Alice or even Ellie, of course, but other people who I thought were my friends or at least liked me. This whole experience is making me lose my faith in human nature.

'Listen to this,' said Karen. She turned to me. 'I bet your mum didn't even have to make any of this up. She just had to steal your diary.' And she started to read from the book.

'"Dear Diary,' she said, in a stupid squeaky voice. 'The competition is hotting up! I've got to work harder. Today Caoimhe chose her victim -- I mean, future boyfriend. At least, that what she hopes! He's a guy who goes to St Joseph's and I've got to admit, he's not bad. In fact, I wish I'd seen him first! But I'm still determined to find the perfect boy for me."'

Karen put down the book for a moment and flicked through the pages, while everyone sniggered along. 'It gets better, everyone. Listen to this. "I know this sounds crazy, but I have a funny feeling about ..." She paused dramatically. '"Wildfire. I really think our group is going to be famous someday. I know I'm not the prettiest girl in the world. I'm not very tall and my eyes are a boring grey colour and my hair's a kind of ordinary wavy brown."' Karen paused again and gestured towards me. And PEOPLE LAUGHED. I hate my class. And my mother. Why couldn't stupid Ruthie have been 5 foot 11 and had black or blonde or red hair? Anything but a wavy brown-haired midget! Anyway, Karen wasn't finished reading aloud. '"But when we're all together and we're all dressed up, I feel gorgeous! I know I can sing too. It's not boasting;

it's just something I've always known. And when we're singing and dancing together, I feel like there's nothing stopping us being pop stars. We just need to get discovered. I wonder if we should enter one of those TV talent shows? After all, it worked for Girls Aloud."'

Karen laughed again. She is very easily amused. 'So, Rebecca,' she sniggered. 'You think you're going to be the next Cheryl Cole, do you?'

I gritted my teeth. 'I know you find this hard to believe, Karen,' I said. 'But that book is actually MADE UP. It's not true.'

'Huh,' said Karen. 'Well, I can't wait to see you and your little chums singing and dancing with, heh heh, Wildfire. Do you get to do a solo?'

'Oh my God, Karen!' I shrieked. 'I am not Ruthie Whatserface!'

Karen looked at me and smirked. I've never hated anyone so much in my life. Not even Mum. Not even Rachel when she read my diary when I was twelve (there wasn't anything particularly scandalous in it, but it was the thought that counts). 'Well, yeah,' she said. 'I suppose I can't imagine you actually doing anything as cool as starting a band. Even a sad girl band.'

And I was so angry that I spoke without thinking properly. Or thinking at all, really.

'Actually,' I said, 'I *am* in a band. And it's nothing like the ridiculous one in the book. We're an indie band. And I'm the drummer.'

Next to me, Alice and Cass froze. I could almost hear them thinking 'oh no ...'

'Yeah, right,' said Karen Rodgers. 'You're the drummer in an indie band. Of course you are. God, you're sad.'

'I'm sad?' I said. 'You're the one who went to the trouble of getting my mum's book and reading it just to annoy me. That's the saddest thing I've ever heard. And yes, I am in a band. With Alice and Cass.'

Karen gave a fake sort of laugh.

'Oh yeah?' she said. 'So what are you called?'

Of course, I didn't know what to say, so I stared at the shelf next to me. And the first thing that caught my eye was a battered old paperback by an author called Deborah something or other called *Hey, Dollface*.

'Hey Dollface!' I said suddenly.

'What?' said Karen.

'What?' said Alice and Cass, but luckily no one seemed to notice that they'd said anything because Karen was doing another stupid loud fake laugh which probably drowned out any other sound in a five-mile radius.

'Yes,' I said. 'That's the name of our band. Not,' I forced a laugh which sounded almost as fake as Karen's, 'Wildfire. I'm sure you'll get to see us at some stage. We'll be playing some gigs eventually.'

I could almost feel Alice and Cass glaring at me. Karen opened her mouth to say something, but then the librarian came in so we all had to hurry into our seats. As I was passing Karen I whispered, 'Thanks for buying Mum's book, by the way. That money will buy me a new set of drumsticks!'

It won't, of course, because writers only get a tiny amount of money for every book they sell, but Karen doesn't know that. And she looked as sick as a pig. Ha!

My triumph was shortlived, of course, because at lunchtime everyone started asking about the band. We sort of acted like we'd been doing it for ages, because we didn't want to admit we've only had one practice.

'Yeah, I got the drums a while ago,' I said, taking my

lunch out of my bag. 'And Alice and Cass have been playing the guitar and the piano for ages.' Well, that's all technically true.

'I can't believe you didn't tell me!' said Ellie.

'Well, we were going to keep it quiet for a while,' said Cass, giving me a meaningful look. Cass is very good at giving meaningful looks. Maybe it's because they are intensified by her glasses. 'We wanted to wait until we were ready to play gigs.'

'So who do you sound like?' asked Jessie McCabe.

Of course, we don't really sound like anyone yet. We've only really played one song, and that was by the Kinks.

'Um, we're still working on our general sound,' I said. Then, of course, Karen, who was sitting at the next desk, had to stick her oar in.

'Well, at least we know you can sing,' she said. 'At least, your alter-ego can. She was boasting about it in this ridiculous book.'

I ignored her and started eating my sandwich.

'Are you going to play any concerts?' asked Ellie. 'You have to tell us if you do.'

'Well, we really want to play gigs,' said Alice, although

to be honest I'm not sure Cass actually does. 'But, um, we're not sure how. I think we're too young to play most places.'

'You should ask Rebecca,' said Karen. 'After all, Wildfire played a concert.'

I rolled my eyes as if I was just mildly amused by Karen's ravings, as opposed to wanting to kill her. This seemed to annoy her because she shut up for a while. And then we went out to sit in the playing field and eat crisps, and I managed to avoid her for the rest of the day.

Alice doesn't really care all that much about everyone knowing about the band, but Cass does. She says she didn't want anyone to know about it until we were amazing musicians and had written loads of songs, rather than three girls who had only had one practice. 'And only two of us can play our instruments properly,' she said. 'No offence.'

'I'm not that bad,' I said.

'Sorry,' said Cass. 'But you know what I mean. It's not that you're bad, you just haven't had much chance to practise.'

'Hmm,' I said. 'Fair enough.'

Anyway, it's done now, and there's nothing we can do to change it, as Alice very sensibly pointed out. She also said everyone will forget about it soon, although that wasn't quite as sensible. No one in our class seems to forget anything. They're like elephants in hideous wine-coloured uniforms. Some of them still go on about the time Jessie accidentally called Frau O'Hara 'Mum' in class and that happened nearly a year ago.

THURSDAY ☾

Have been practising the drums on the sofa cushions. I think I am getting better. In fact, I know I'm getting better. You just have to learn to relax your wrists. Of course, the pedal thing still freaks me out a bit, but I'll figure it out. And I don't really need to play a big bass drum very often (I hope). I'm kind of avoiding playing the cymbals for the same reason. Also, it turns out that playing the drums (or cushions) is very good way of letting out your rage. Obviously I have had lots of things to be angry about recently (Mum, Mrs Harrington, Karen Rodgers, Vanessa Finn) and after a good bash I do feel much better.

To my amazement, I am not the only person who thinks I am getting better. Dad came in today while I was drumming away on the sofa and said, 'Wow, Bex; you sound like a real drummer!'

Maybe I really have found my calling.

After reading *Pride and Prejudice* (which was very good. Especially as Elizabeth escaped her embarrassing mother in the end), I am in the mood for more old-fashioned books about people with horrible parents. Rachel gave me *Jane Eyre*, which was also written in the olden days. It is okay so far. Jane Eyre is an orphan which frankly doesn't sound so bad to me right now. Although I suppose Dad isn't that bad. Some of the time.

FRIDAY ✯

Vanessa Finn is being so nice to me I'm starting to feel a bit sorry for her friend Caroline. Today she asked me if I wanted to sit with her for lunch, ignoring poor old Caroline. In our class we don't go around asking people to join us for lunch, and I was already eating my sandwiches (wholemeal bread, cheese, ham and lettuce) and drinking a carton of juice (apple) with Cass and Alice, as usual. So that was weird anyway. Caroline just sat there, looking hurt. I politely said that I was having lunch with Cass and Alice, and Vanessa gave me a sugary smile and offered me some of her chocolate brownie. But I didn't want to take any of it. I'm afraid she has ulterior motives. I just wish I knew what they were.

And I had another conversation with Paperboy this evening. But I'm not sure if that was a good thing or not. I was at home practising the drums, as is my wont these days, and when the door rang I shouted 'I'll get it!' and walked very calmly into the kitchen, got the paper money from the counter, and walked slowly out to the door (I ignored Rachel sniggering and saying, 'Oh, Bex is answering the door at this time on a Friday, what a surprise'). Then I took a deep breath, smiled, and opened the door. And there he was, looking as lovely as ever. Oh, he's so tall. I have to lean my head back to look up at him, even when he's standing a step lower than me.

'Hi,' I said. I held out the cash. 'Here you go.'

'Thanks,' he said, in a friendly way. 'Did you manage to

stay out of the papers this week?'

Without thinking, I said, 'Well, no, not exactly.' As soon as I said it I wished I'd kept my mouth shut. Or rather, lied. If he hadn't seen the shorts photo, what on earth was I doing telling him about it? It was better if he never knew anything about it But it was too late now. And then it was like I was possessed. I couldn't stop talking. 'My mother did an interview with a newspaper and gave them a photo of me and my sister when we were little,' I said. 'We were wearing ridiculous shorts. It was pretty embarrassing.' Which is why, of course, I am telling you. WHAT IS WRONG WITH ME?

But Paperboy laughed in quite a nice way. 'Wow, you really are famous,' he said. 'I'm not sure that I, a humble paperboy, should be allowed talk to you.'

I should have thought of something clever or funny to say to that, but of course I didn't, so I just laughed like a crazy person and he grinned and went off.

I wonder if he thinks I actually am a crazy person? Or at least a sad idiot who appears in the paper by accident all the time.

He was quite friendly though. And he was joking with

me in a nice way, not a sniggering way. That was pretty cool.

Hmmm.

SATURDAY ★

I don't want to write about this but I suppose I have to. Something horrible happened today. We had an early band practice because Alice had to go and visit some relatives, and afterwards Cass and I went into town on the bus. Cass had to buy a birthday present for her brother in some stupid sports shop and she said she knew it wasn't fair to make me go there, so we split up and said we'd meet in half an hour. I went off to potter around the shops, even though I couldn't really afford to buy anything, and when I was coming out of Tower Records, Paperboy was coming in. We almost walked into each other in the doorway and when I realized it was him my stomach turned over with excitement and happiness. We just stared at each other and I was starting to say hello when I realised there was someone with him. A girl. She was tall-ish (taller than me, anyway) with brown hair and she was wearing a really nice coat and had a cool bag. She was quite pretty, I suppose.

I froze for a split second and then said, 'Oh, hi!' I hope I sounded casual. I have a horrible feeling I didn't. He looked a bit awkward and said smiled and said, 'Hey.' And the girl sort of looked at me funny. If we'd been in the street, I'd have just kept walking but we were still in the doorway so there was a stupid awkward bit where we all moved out of each other's way in the same direction until finally I broke free and sort of bounded out into Wicklow Street. I said, 'Um, bye then,' and he waved and said, 'See ya,' and the girl just looked at me blankly, and then I walked down the street as fast as I could and I wanted to die. I wished I didn't have to meet Cass at all because I just wanted to be on my own. I sort of wandered around the streets near the George's Street Arcade until it was time to meet her, trying not to cry. We went for a hot chocolate and I told her what had happened. I tried not to show how awful I felt. Cass was all 'oh no, he's taken!' but she didn't seem to really care. And I do care. And I feel really embarrassed for caring.

I keep running it over and over in my head. I wish I

knew whether they were holding hands or not. I mean I wish I knew that they weren't – right now I think they weren't but I can't be sure. Not that it makes any difference. I'm clutching at straws. I wish I could tell myself that she was his sister or his cousin or just his friend but I don't want to give myself false hope. I feel so, so, so stupid. I've spent the last few weeks thinking about him so much, I really thought there was at least a possibility that there was something in it. I can't believe I was all happy and hopeful about him last night. I can't believe we were practically engaged in my dreams. I wish he liked me. I wish I knew him.

SUNDAY

Here's something really shameful – I keep wondering whether Paperboy looked awkward when we met because he didn't want me to know that he had a girlfriend. Because he likes me. But probably he just looked awkward because he thinks I'm just a silly little girl he bumps into every week when he's doing his job and he doesn't want to have to see me in public. I hope he doesn't know I like him. If he did and felt sorry for me I would die. It's the worst thing I can possibly imagine. Although he probably feels sorry for me anyway, with my unwanted fame. God, I'm so pathetic.

LATER

I rang Alice and told her everything, including how crappy I felt (I didn't tell her about my shameful hope that Paperboy secretly loves me). I don't know why it was easier than talking to Cass. I suppose it was partly because, after the first excitement, I don't think Alice really cared about Paperboy. She preferred the boy who (still) goes past us on his bike on Calderwood Road. He actually sort of smiled at us the other day so perhaps she's on the right track. But also it was because we have been friends for much longer than me and Cass, and although I do get on really well with Cass and she is very funny and I probably have more in common with her than I do with Alice, sometimes I feel that perhaps Alice understands me better, in a more serious way, not just about liking the same books and music and

TV programmes and stuff like that. So yeah, I told her, and she was really nice about it, and said she understood, and told me about how once she saw Bike Boy exchanging waves with a girl in a St Mary's uniform when we were on our way into school, and I hadn't seen anything so she acted normally until we got there and then she went into the toilets and cried. Anyway, I felt a bit better after I talked to her.

MONDAY

I keep forgetting about Paperboy and his stupid girlfriend (it actually gives me a horrible pain in my stomach to write that) and then I remember and feel sick in my tummy. School is so boring, I have plenty of time to think about it. I was in such a daze in maths that I didn't even notice that Ellie and Jessie were having a competition to see who could tip their seat back the furthest without falling over until Jessie actually did fall over and Mrs Condren spent the rest of the class telling us how we were meant to be grown-up now and it was disgraceful to see fourteen-year-old girls acting like babies.

TUESDAY

As if I didn't have enough to annoy me at the moment, Vanessa Finn kept going on at me again today. What is up with her recently? I ended up having to sit next to her in German because Cass and I were late for class and there weren't two free seats beside each other so Frau O'Hara ordered me to sit next to Vanessa. Anyway, we were meant to be practising talking about our favourite TV programmes 'auf Deutsch' but Vanessa kept talking about this ginormous birthday party she's planning and asking me what I thought about it.

'I haven't decided whether to arrive on a big pink tank or a pink horse. What do you think?'

What I thought was that she was a total lunatic but I just said, 'Um, where are you going to get a pink horse?'

'Oh, we're just going to dye a white one,' she said, as if this was a perfectly normal thing to do. Perhaps it is, for her. Perhaps she has a whole stable of horses of every colour.

'And, well, where are you going to get a tank? Isn't that, like, illegal?'

'Dad has a friend who's an army officer,' said Vanessa. 'He said we could just borrow one for the day.'

'Really?' I said.

'Yah. And we can paint it pink as long as we paint it grey or green or whatever boring colour it's meant to be afterwards.'

It was so mad I have to admit I was kind of fascinated.

'Are you going to, like, ride through the streets in it? In a tank?' I asked.

'Yeah,' she said. 'I'll be, you know, looking out in the top in my new outfit. Waving at people.'

I always knew Vanessa was a bit peculiar and annoying, but I thought she was basically harmless. Now it sounds like she wants to be Hitler. Only more pink. Anyway, Frau O'Hara came along then so she had to shut up (in English at least). But she kept going in German. She was of course meant to be talking about telly programmes but I'm pretty sure she was still talking about the party (it is hard to tell as her German is even worse than mine). I heard the word 'Pferd' which means horse so maybe she is just obsessed with horses in general? Although she also said something about a 'Fest'. As soon as the class ended she started talking about the tank as well (or Panzer, as I believe they are called 'auf Deutsch'), but I said I had to go to the loo urgently and ran away (it was the only excuse I could think of). To be honest Vanessa's mad party should be a distraction, but at the moment I can't think about anything but Paperboy and that horrible girl. Why did I go in to Tower on Saturday? If I hadn't seen them I wouldn't feel so awful now. I mean, I know that it doesn't change the fact that he's going out with her (IF he is) but at least then I wouldn't know about it. Every time I think about it I feel sick. And very, very sad.

THURSDAY ☾

We had an extra band practice after school today. Alice asked her mum to let us do it, to cheer me up, which was very kind of her. I'm not sure it actually worked, because now I'm back home again and I feel miserable, but I have to admit that when we were actually practising it did distract me from my misery for a while.

Maybe I should start writing poetry. I could turn my sadness into great literature.

LATER

Nothing rhymes with Paperboy.

EVEN LATER

If only I knew his real name. Although it's probably something unrhymable, like Jonathan. Not that he looks like a Jonathan. I actually can't imagine what his name might be. He doesn't look like an anything, if you know what I mean. I mean, you wouldn't look at him and think, 'There's a Dave,' or 'There's a Rory.'

Anyway, there isn't any point in finding out what his name is. I'll probably never talk to him about anything but newspapers. And I'm not sure I even want to do that anymore.

FRIDAY ✯

I feel a bit funny. In a good way. Something very weird and potentially very, very good has happened. I don't quite know what to think about it. I was really jittery when I came home from school because I knew Paperboy was going to call in a few hours. And I didn't know whether to leave Rachel or Mum to answer the door or to brave it and do it myself. A part of me really wanted to see him but another part of me couldn't bear the idea. But then I thought that if I didn't answer the door, he'd think I was hiding from him (and he would be right). And then I felt ashamed of myself for being stupid enough to think that he'd even notice, or that he even remembers Saturday.

I decided to distract myself by practising my drums. Rachel was up in her room, Dad wasn't home from work yet and Mum was in her study, so I put on some music and started drumming away on the cushions. I was hoping I might get so lost in music that I would forget about the impending arrival of Paperboy but of course I didn't and I kept looking over at the clock. When it hit six o'clock my stomach was churning and when the door rang at half six I thought I was going to get sick. But I yelled 'I'll get it' (my voice came out a bit weird) and ran out to the door, still holding my drumsticks (and if I'm being totally honest with myself, and I should be if I want this diary to be an accurate description of my life when I look back on it in my old age, I have to admit this: I didn't put the drumsticks down before going out because I hoped he would be impressed by the fact I play the drums. GOD I'M SO SAD).

Anyway, I kind of flung open the door and there he was. I'd been thinking about him so much all week that it was a shock to see him in the flesh, in different clothes. In my head he looked exactly as he'd looked on Saturday. I felt my throat go all dry and I swallowed before I said, 'Oh, hi, I'll get the money.' But before I could get away, the (possibly – I don't want to tempt fate) cool thing happened.

Paperboy said, 'Um, I'm sorry about Saturday.'

I sort of stared at him and, after what seemed like about five years but was probably only about five seconds, said, 'What for?'

Paperboy let out a long breath. 'Em, I think I was a bit rude. By accident.'

'No you weren't,' I said, but Paperboy was on a roll. 'I'd just bumped into my ex outside Tower and it was all a bit weird because we haven't really seen each other since I broke up with her and when we met you I was kind of surprised. So I might have acted a bit weird. Or rude. But just because I was surprised to see you there.'

'So was I,' I said. 'It was weird seeing you, um, out of context. I mean, not doing your whole ... paper thing.' But while I said this I was just thinking. 'His ex! HIS EX! HIS EX!!!' and I thought I was going to die of happiness.

'So yeah, I'm sorry if I seemed a bit, you know, off,' said Paperboy, looking a bit awkward. Neither of us said anything for a moment. Then he suddenly looked surprised and pleased. 'Hey, are those drumsticks?'

'Um, yeah,' I said. 'I'm in a band.' I didn't add 'and we can't really play any songs!' because that would not have been impressive. And Paperboy looked kind of impressed. 'Really?' he said. 'Wow, that's brilliant. What are you called?'

For a moment I wished we weren't committed to our new name. But we are.

'We're called ... Hey Dollface,' I said. 'But we haven't been a band for very long. We're just starting out, really.'

'Cool,' said Paperboy with a grin. 'I like the name. It sounds like something out of a trashy fifties' movie.' I have never seen any trashy fifties' movies, so I hope this is a good thing. It sounds pretty cool anyway. And Paperboy wasn't finished.

'Hey, have you heard about the Battle of the Bands thing in the Knitting Factory?' he said. 'It's for under-eighteens, so it's on a Saturday afternoon. It's in about three weeks, I think. My friend Johnny is entering his band.'

'Wow!' I said. 'That sounds brilliant.' And it did. Although I can't imagine that we will be good enough to enter a battle in three weeks, unless we want to totally humiliate ourselves. And frankly, I've had more than enough humiliation for a lifetime recently. I can't take any more.

'Yeah, you should enter,' said Paperboy. 'You can look it up online. I went last year and it was good fun. It's an easy way to play a first gig. And you don't have to worry about whether the audience likes you or not, because they're all just worried about their own sets. Although that may not be ideal either. Am I talking too much?'

'No,' I said.

He was smiling. He has such a nice smile. One side of his mouth seems to go up a bit more than the other. I could look at him all day. God, I hope I wasn't staring too madly at him. 'Anyway, I'd better go and harass some more of your neighbours for money. It's just something I like to do on a Friday evening.' He raised his hand in farewell. 'Let me know if you enter the Knitting Factory yoke.'

'Yeah,' I said. 'Um, thanks!' And he sort of waved and went off and I waved a drumstick at him as he went down the drive. I hope he knew I was waving goodbye and not, like, threatening him with a drumstick beating or something. Then I closed the door, ran upstairs, ran into my room and shrieked at the top of my voice in pure, pure joy. I jumped up and down and then fell on the bed smiling from ear to ear. I'm still smiling now. I know I'm being stupid and it doesn't mean anything really but Paperboy doesn't have a girlfriend after all AND I had a proper conversation with him AND he thought it was cool that I'm in a band AND he said, 'Let me know' if we enter the competition which means he wants to talk to me again (or at least he isn't totally terrified of the thought). And nothing might come of this and I might never talk to him again but right now I am very, very happy.

LATER

I can't believe I talked to him for that long. It was like a dream. 'Let me know if you enter the Knitting Factory yoke.' Squeeeeeeee!!!

SATURDAY ★

Band practice today! Cass's mum gave me and her a lift to Alice's house. I didn't say anything about Paperboy or the Battle of the Bands on the way because (a) I couldn't talk properly about Paperboy in front of Cass's mum and (b) I wanted to make a grand announcement to my bandmates and you can't make a grand announcement twice. So I waited until we were in the practice room and told them all.

Cass said, 'Oh my God, I'm so jealous! You bitch!' But I don't think she meant it. Unless she is a very good actor. She seemed genuinely quite pleased for me. If she does really like him she is being very noble.

Alice looked delighted and played a very loud power chord in my honour. And then she revealed that she has actually written a song. Well, some chords that make a song. It doesn't have an actual tune or words or anything. But it has a riff and she played it and it was actually pretty good. Very choppy and poppy and sharp. I started drumming along and Cass played a squelchy, funky sort of bass line and it didn't sound bad at all.

'You know,' I said, 'if we tighten that up and make up a tune and everything, we really could enter this Battle of the Bands.'

'Are you serious about that?' said Cass.

'Of course I am!' I said. 'Why do you think I mentioned it earlier?'

'Well,' said Cass. 'I thought it was just part of the Paperboy conversation. I mean, I didn't think you actually wanted to enter it. I thought you were just pleased he thought we should do it.'

'Of course I want to enter it!' I said. 'Don't you?'

'I think I want to enter it,' said Alice.

'Well, I don't,' said Cass. 'It's in three weeks! We're not good enough!'

'Oh come on,' I said. 'I looked up the details online last night and you only need to play two songs. So we could do this one and a cover.'

There was silence as Cass thought this over.

'Just think, Cass,' I said. 'All of us rocking out on stage ... everyone cheering us on ...'

'Everyone laughing at us, more like,' said Cass.

'Cheering!' I said.

'What,' said Alice suddenly, 'is the point of us being in a band if we only ever play in here? I mean, why are we doing it?'

'The love of music,' said Cass loftily.

'If it was just the love of music, we could just do it on our own, not in a band. We need to play in front of other people! We need an audience.'

'Just imagine what nice boys would be there and how

impressed they'd be,' I said. 'Not that that's the most important thing, of course. But still!'

'Huh,' said Cass.

'Just think about it,' said Alice, the skilful diplomat. 'Let's practise a bit more first.'

So we kept going with the song. Alice started singing a tune over the chords and we all offered suggestions. Then we all started singing it together, like one of those sixties' girl groups. It's quite hard to hear each other over the noise of the instruments – we can't use the microphones because we don't have enough amplifiers – but we turned the volume down on the guitar and keyboard and I tried to drum quietly. Alice and I worked out a sort of harmony so we sounded like a little choir. Of course, we didn't have any lyrics, we just sang 'bap-bap-bap' instead. After a while it actually, seriously, started coming together. It sounded like actual music. I couldn't believe it.

'Wow, Alice,' I said. 'You've actually written a song.'

'We've written a song,' said Alice. 'You two came up with your own drumming and keyboard bits and we all made the tune. And we're all singing. I just put the chords together.'

We looked at each other in amazement. We wrote a song! A brand new song, that didn't exist before this afternoon! It was an excellent feeling. We played it from beginning to end with only a few wonky mistakes and at the end of it Cass said, 'Okay, okay, let's do it.'

'Seriously?' squeaked Alice.

'Yeah, go on. Let's make a fool of ourselves in front of everyone we know. You know half our class will turn up just to laugh at us, don't you?'

They probably will, but I don't care. We're entering the competition!

MONDAY

I had a brainwave and took home little bits of my drums so I can practise at home. I took the snare drum, which is the small rattly drum, and the bass drum pedal (I am making it hit the side of the sofa instead of a drum. Good old sofa, what would my musical career be without it? It's practically a drum kit now. Although Mum and Dad aren't too happy about this. Mum said I'll destroy the sofa bashing away like that but I told her I don't actually hit it that hard. I am a skilled artiste, after all). So anyway, I'm sure I'll be able to manage the whole pedal business by the time of the competition. Which, I might add, we have officially entered. I did it last night. I just had to fill in a form online saying how many of us there were, and what instruments we played, and how many singers we had. We told Ellie and Emma about it and made them promise not to tell everyone else.

'You've got to let us come, though,' said Ellie. 'I mean, surely you want someone cheering you on?'

It's true, we do. But only if we're good. Which we may not be. But we don't want to admit that. Oh, being in a band is complicated.

'Well, yes, we do,' said Cass. 'But it might all be very boring for you. I mean, there are going to be loads of bands playing and I'm pretty sure most of them will be crap.'

'Oh, that's okay,' said Emma. 'It'll be fun anyway.'

'Well, um, thanks,' said Alice. And that was that. I suppose it doesn't really matter if Ellie and Emma see us making fools out of ourselves. As long as they don't tell anyone.

To my amazement, Rachel says she wants to come too.

'It'll be hilarious,' she said. 'The three of you up on the stage. I hope they'll have room for the sofa, seeing as that seems to be your instrument of choice. Admit it, you don't play the drums out in Alice's garage at all. You're just in her sitting room bashing the couch.'

'Ha ha,' I said. 'I'm not having you there laughing at us.'

Rachel sighed. 'I'm only joking,' she said. 'Well, sort of. I do think you're probably better at playing the sofa than the drums. But I actually do want to go and cheer you on. I'm not a total bitch, you know.'

Hmmm. Maybe she isn't. She did arrange for me to get the drums in the first place, after all.

'Huh,' I said. 'Okay, I suppose you can come. If you behave yourself.'

Rachel rolled her eyes. 'God, talk about ungrateful. I'm not sure I want to go now.'

'Alright, alright,' I said. 'I do want you to come. Thanks.'

'That's more like it,' said Rachel smugly, and ran out of the room before I could throw a drumstick at her (I did anyway, but it just hit the door frame. She is very good at dodging missiles. So am I, come to that. We've spent a lot of the last fourteen years throwing things at each other).

WEDNESDAY

Extra band practice today! My mum was going to see some friend who lives in Malahide so she gave me, Cass and Alice a lift out to Alice's house (with the bits of drums I took home the other day) after school and then collected me and Cass afterwards. Alice is in a very good mood because something quite cool happened on our way to school today. We were walking down Calderwood Road and then Alice said, 'We should use this opportunity to have a band practice.'

'How?' I said. 'Do you have a guitar and a drum kit in your school bag?'

Alice sighed. 'No, I mean we should practise singing the song. It's not like there's anyone else around. We need to come up with lyrics, anyway.'

'Oh, all right,' I said, and we started singing. Not very

loudly, I might add. It was quite fun, singing as we marched along, and then I noticed a familiar figure cycling along quite near us. It was Alice's dream boy on a bike. And he was looking right at us in a friendly way.

'Hey,' he said cheerfully, 'you're not bad. You should start a band!'

He looked like he was about to cycle off, and then Alice, sensible, shy Alice, looked straight at him and said, 'We already have. I'm the guitarist.'

Bike Boy looked genuinely impressed. He was cycling very, very slowly. 'Seriously?'

We both nodded. 'And she plays drums,' said Alice.

'Wow,' said Bike Boy. 'Well, good luck. With the band, I mean.'

And he cycled off. Alice and I just stared at each other with our mouths open until he'd made it to the end of the road and turned the corner and then we both shrieked. But not too loudly.

'Alice, I think being in a band is good for you,' I said. 'I bet you wouldn't have dared speak to Bike Boy a few weeks ago.'

'I think you're right,' said Alice. And her good mood

lasted for the rest of the day, even when Miss Kelly started waffling on about peak oil and how she hoped we all liked cycling because by the time we were forty only billionaires would be able to use cars.

The practice went quite well too. We have written some very basic lyrics for our song. We weren't really sure what to write about, because song lyrics should be about significant romantic life experiences, and, to be honest, none of us have actually had any yet. All we've had is 'fancying boys we don't really know properly', and as Cass said thoughtfully, 'I don't think you can really write a song about that without sounding like a stalker.'

So we kept going with the 'bap-bap-bap's' until Alice said, 'Why don't we write about the fuss about your mum's book, Bex?'

'What?' I said. 'We can't write about that. It'd sound insane.'

'Yes,' said Cass. She started singing to the tune of our nameless song.

'My mother wrote a book
It was bad

And my teacher

Has gone mad ...'

'I didn't mean literally about your mum's book,' said Alice. 'I mean, we could write about someone wanting to show the world what she was really like. Which is what you want to do now everyone thinks Ruthie O'Reilly is you.'

'Hmmm, that is a good idea,' said Cass.

'Everyone doesn't really think Ruthie O'Reilly is me,' I said. 'Do they?'

'Here, listen to this,' said Alice. She started playing the chords of the song. Then she started to sing.

'They think they know me

The real me

Just how wrong can

People be?'

'Wow, that's not totally terrible,' said Cass.

'It's really not,' I said. I sat down behind my drum kit. 'Let's try it all together.'

And we did. And it sounded kind of good. We came up with some more lyrics (Alice wrote them all down so we wouldn't forget anything) and I think it works. Every so often Alice will mess up a chord or I'll drop a drumstick, but we managed to play both songs from beginning to end lots of times without any HUGE mistakes.

'We actually sound like a real band,' said Cass. 'At least, a real band who can only play very, very short concerts because we only have two songs.'

'That's all we need to be able to play for the Battle of the Bands,' I said.

By the end of the practice we were all in such a good mood, including me, that I forgot how much I hate my mother at the moment and talked quite cheerfully to her in the car on the way home. After we dropped off Cass, she said, 'So, am I forgiven?'

Then, of course, I remembered all the terrible things that have happened at school recently.

'No,' I said. 'I'll never forgive you. That book has ruined my life!'

And I didn't say anything for the rest of the journey. Mum looked a bit sad and I felt slightly guilty, but then I remembered Karen Rodgers sneering at me and reading out bits of the book and said nothing. I am not very good at being aloof and stand-offish, though. When we got home we all watched a funny programme on telly and although I was determined to sit very straight at the end of the couch and not join in everyone's foolish laughter, I sort of forgot after a few minutes. Well, it really was funny. And being aloof isn't much fun.

I still haven't forgiven Mum, of course.

FRIDAY ✯

Or as I like to think of it now, Paperboy Day. Although it wasn't, because I didn't get to see him. I can't believe it. I was in need of some cheering up as school was extremely boring. When Mrs Harrington isn't harassing me and acting like a lunatic, she is still a terrible teacher. When I think of the way Ms Ardagh used to make English classes so fun, I want to cry. It used to be my favourite class, and now I dread it. Luckily Mrs Harrington didn't single me out for any more public humiliation today. She just droned on about *Great Expectations* for what seemed like about six years. And every other class was just as dull, although German managed to be boring AND weird. I ended up having to sit next to Vanessa Finn again and she kept writing me notes about her ridiculous party like we were best pals. Apparently she is having a dress made for her out of solid gold or something. I don't know, my brain started to switch off after the first sentence. I can't believe her parents are spending so much money on this craziness. Hasn't she heard that we're all meant to be tightening our belts, whatever that means? I'm pretty sure we're not meant to be splashing out on gold dresses and tanks.

So yes, today was not a good day. And then I missed Paperboy! Mum said it was okay for me to practise my bits of drum in the house as long as I did it up in my room rather than in the sitting room with my beloved sofa. So when I came home from school I thought, correctly, that a bit of drumming would make me feel better. I decided to put on some music to drum along to and I was enjoying myself very much when the door opened and Rachel came in, all dressed up like a dog's dinner because she was going out with Tom.

'What do you want?' I said. 'I'm practising my drums!'

'Yes, I know,' said Rachel. 'I can hear you all over the house. I thought I'd let you know that that Paperboy of yours is looking very well this evening.'

I nearly dropped my drumsticks.

'When did you see him?' I cried.

'Just now,' said Rachel smugly. 'He just called for the paper money.'

'But ... but it's only half-five!' I said. 'And I didn't hear the door bell.'

'Well, that's because you were making all that noise,' said Rachel. 'You can probably hear that racket half way down the street.'

I scowled. 'You sound like Mum, 'I said. 'And I can't believe I missed him.' I have given up pretending I don't fancy him to Rachel, because my pretending just seemed to amuse her. 'He's the only boy I like and I only get to see him once a week.'

Rachel sighed. 'Okay,' she said. 'Would it make you feel any better if I told you that he asked after you?'

This time I really did drop my drumsticks. 'Really?' I squeaked.

'Yes!' said Rachel. 'Well, sort of. I answered the door and he looked sort of surprised. He's probably so used to you racing out to the door and panting at him every week, he doesn't realise anyone else lives here. Anyway, he said he was here for the paper money, and I said, "Oh, you're a bit earlier than usual, I'll have to go and get it," and he said something about a change of schedule and I went off to get the cash from Mum. And when I came back he pointed upstairs and said, "Um, is that your sister playing the drums?" And I said, "I'm afraid I don't have a sister, but we are looking after a poor idiot orphan, and every Friday night we let her hit some saucepans with a wooden spoon."'

'What?' I shrieked.

'Oh, calm down, you fool, I didn't say that,' said Rachel. 'I was a perfect sister, actually. I said, "Yes, that's her. She's not bad."'

'Did you really?' I asked, rather surprised.

'Yes,' said Rachel. 'Seriously, I did! And he said, "Yeah, she's very good," and looked a little bit impressed. And I said, "She's in a band, you know. They're entering some battle of the bands next week," and he said, "Oh, cool, I'll see them then." And that was it.'

'What do you mean, that was it?' I said.

'I mean he said bye and went off. What else was he going to do, come up and start a drum circle with you?'

'How did he look when he said he was going to see us in the battle of the bands?' I said. 'Did he look like he was just saying it out of politeness or did he look like he actually wanted to see us?'

'Oh, God, I don't know,' said Rachel. 'I'm not obsessed with him like you. He looked perfectly friendly, and like I said, he really did look quite impressed by your awful drum bashing, God knows why. So I think you can assume he's at least slightly interested in seeing your ridiculous band. He must be mad.'

'But what ...' I began, but Rachel cut me off. 'I'm off to see Tom,' she said. 'And I've told you all I can about your beloved. So if you want to analyse his every word, go round to Cass's house.'

But I couldn't, because she's at another one of her brother's football matches. Her parents are making them all go for family bonding. Cass says they're the most boring things ever and she just stands at the side of the pitch and listens to her iPod. It's not so bad at this time of year, but it's really awful in winter. So I rang Alice instead. We spent quite a lot of time trying to figure out what Paperboy's statement could mean.

'I hate to say it,' said Alice, 'but it might just mean that he's going to be at the battle of the bands. And no more.'

'But is he going to see us or his friends?' I said.

'Well, in fairness, Bex, I'm pretty sure he's going mostly to see his friends,' said Alice. 'I mean, it'd be a bit odd if he was just there to see us. He barely knows you.'

'I know, I know,' I said. And of course I do know. But it's nice to imagine that he actively wants to see us. Even if he probably doesn't.

SATURDAY ✶

No practice today, we're having it tomorrow instead. So I just stayed at home. I didn't even go into town or round to Cass's house. It should have been boring but actually it is sometimes quite nice not having to do anything. I liked knowing that I could call over to Cass if I wanted to, so I didn't feel like I was being forced to stay home on my own against my will. I just sort of pottered around the house reading and watching telly and thinking about Paperboy. Rachel was over at Tom's and Mum and Dad were out shopping at a garden centre (oh, what fascinating lives grown-ups lead. Seriously, if I ever have the urge to go to a garden centre, aka the most boring place on earth full of giant terracotta pots and metal benches, I hope someone shoots me), so I had the house to myself. I made a sort of nest for myself on the couch and settled in with Bumpers, a big mug of hot chocolate, a pile of books and magazines, some DVD box sets and the TV remote. It was like going to a fancy spa, only less healthy. By the time Mum and Dad came back with a spade or a big bag of compost or something else equally ridiculous, I was feeling very relaxed and grown-up.

'Welcome home, Mother and Father,' I said politely. 'Did you have a nice afternoon? Would you like a cup of tea?'

Mum and Dad looked at me suspiciously.

'What have you done?' said Dad. 'Did you break something?'

Honestly! There's no point in acting like an adult around here, they insist on treating me like a five-year-old.

SUNDAY

Band practice! All my drumming at home is paying off. I am no longer the weakest link, at least as far as my actual playing is concerned. In fact, we're all playing quite well at the moment. Which is good as we now have less than two weeks to the competition. But there is still a problem.

'We really need to, I dunno, show off more on stage,' said Cass.

This was so unlike the way she usually talks about the band I put my hand on her forehead.

'Cass, are you feverish?' I said. 'You're sounding like your old self, not the person who practically starts crying every time you plug your keyboard in.'

Cass shrugged. 'We have to work on our showmanship,' she said.

'Our what?' I said. 'Cass, we're not doing some huge arena spectacular. There won't be time for any costume changes.'

'I know,' said Cass. 'But we can't just get up on stage

and just stand there like ... like lemons. We've got to do something.'

'We're not doing any dancing,' I said quickly. 'I'm not doing anything that might look like Ruthie O'Reilly and Wildfire.'

'I didn't mean dancing,' said Cass. 'I mean, when would we dance? You're sitting down and Alice is weighed down by her guitar. And I'm not dancing on my own.'

'You're certainly not,' said Alice. 'You'd look mad.'

'But we need to do something,' said Cass. 'We need to, I dunno, play with a bit of pizzazz.'

'Pizz-what?' said Alice.

'We do play with pizzazz!' I said. 'We're very enthusiastic.'

'But we spend most our time looking down at our instruments,' said Cass.

'That's just because we're concentrating,' said Alice. 'Which we seriously need to do, as you well know.'

'But it looks boring!' cried Cass. 'We have to do something! We have to look at the audience at least.'

'All right,' I said. 'Let's try playing and not looking at our instruments. Will that please you, Lady Gaga?'

'Huh,' said Cass, but we gave it a try. We played without looking at our instruments once. It turned out to be very difficult. Cass and Alice weren't too awful, actually, but I kept making mistakes. In fact, to be honest, there was more mistake than actual song. I kept missing the cymbals.

'Well, I suppose we've both been playing our instruments for much longer than you,' said Alice kindly. 'You can sort of do it instinctively after a while.'

'Maybe you could concentrate on your drums and just look up at the audience every so often,' said Cass.

And that will have to do. There's no way I'm going to become an amazing sightless drummer in less than two weeks.

I'm not bad when I'm actually hitting them, though. Which is something.

MONDAY

Oh my God. I have discovered why Vanessa Finn has been so weirdly nice to me. You know the way she's been going on about her insane birthday party all the time? Well, it turns out that she's applied to be on that telly programme 'My Big Birthday Bash', the one about horrible spoiled brats and their ridiculously fancy birthday parties. And she thinks that because I have recently been (against my will, of course) in the public eye, being friends with me will impress the judges. I can't believe it! She was just using me! Imagine if I'd actually liked talking about tanks and pink ponies and I thought we were becoming best mates. I'd be really hurt now. Instead I am just annoyed.

The whole thing came out at lunchtime today. Cass and Alice and I were sitting under the coats in the cloakroom talking about what we'd wear on stage during the competition – and how great our song is going to be by then. I think we should dress up in really amazing outfits, but Alice says we should just go for laid-back cool.

'What exactly does that mean?' I said.

'Jeans and t-shirts or cool but, like, not too dressy tops,' said Alice.

'But that's what we always wear!' said Cass. 'We can't go on stage looking like we've just gone into town on a Saturday afternoon!'

'Well, we'll be wearing make-up and stuff,' said Alice.

'And we'll do our hair really nicely.'

'Huh,' said Cass. 'Easy for you. You've got proper hair. Look at me and Bex, we've basically got wavy mops on our heads.'

'Oh, thanks,' I said. 'Speak for yourself, mop-head.'

It was then we heard voices coming from the other side of the coats. It was Vanessa and her minion, Caroline.

'So when are they coming to interview you?' said Caroline.

'In a week or two,' said Vanessa. 'But I have to have loads of the arrangements for the party sorted out by then, so they know exactly what to expect.'

We looked at each other and raised our eyebrows. Who could possibly want to interview Vanessa? Maybe she was auditioning to be a southsider and they were trying to see if they'd let her move across the Liffey.

'There's no way they'll turn you down, Nessa,' said Caroline. 'You've got such amazing ideas. And everything's nearly sorted now.'

'Well, I have worked very hard,' said Vanessa. 'I just need my USP.'

'What's a USP?' said Caroline.

'A Unique Selling Point,' said Vanessa. 'Something no one else will have. That's why I want Rebecca to come.'

We all stared at each other in amazement on the other side of the coats.

'I'm still not exactly sure ...' Caroline began.

'She's basically a celebrity,' said Vanessa. 'I mean, she's been in loads of newspapers. Did you know her mother is some famous writer? Like, properly famous? She's been interviewed on the 'Late Late Show' and even British telly and everything. I had absolutely no idea.'

'Well, she never talks about it,' said Caroline.

'Yah, I know,' said Vanessa. 'It's amazing. Anyway, I'm going to tell the 'My Big Birthday Bash' researchers about her. Once they find out one of my friends is famous, they won't be able to resist. Reality TV producers love people with celebrity parents. They'll go wild.'

'They'll go wild anyway,' said Caroline loyally. 'But ... um, will Rebecca go along with it?'

'Oh, she totally will,' said Vanessa. 'I've been telling her all about my plans and she was really interested. And I've been complimenting her all the time. She and her friends aren't used to being praised by someone like me. It'll have gone straight to her head.'

That was it. I couldn't take any more. I jumped up and shoved my head through the coats. Vanessa and Caroline both shrieked.

'I can't believe you!' I roared. 'First of all, I'm not a celebrity, you lunatic, and second of all, there's no way on earth I'm going to help you get on that ridiculous programme!'

'It's not ridiculous!' said Vanessa, who seemed to have quickly got over the shock of my head popping out at them from between the coats. Caroline, on the other hand, looked like she was going to faint or have a heart attack.

'It so is,' I said. 'And there is absolutely no way I will have anything to do with it. Is this why you've been so nice to me recently?'

'No,' said Vanessa. 'I'm just a naturally giving person.'

'Oh my God,' I said. 'Listen, Vanessa. Even if you paid me, even if you ... if you HYPNOTISED me, I would never go on that programme. And I'm not going to your mental birthday party.'

'It's not mental, as you put it,' said Vanessa. 'It's going to be amazing. I got that tank from my dad's friend, by the way. AND the pink pony.'

'A pink pony?' said Cass from behind the coats. 'Are you a wizard?'

'It's going to be dyed, obviously,' said Vanessa as if she were talking to an idiot. 'And it's going to parade in front of me as the pink tank goes along. And I'm going to be waving from the tank. Everyone's going to be talking about it.'

'They'll be talking about it all right,' said Cass.

'Look, Rebecca,' said Vanessa, in a sensible two-adults-having-a-heart-to-heart way. 'You don't have to make your mind up now. The researcher's going to be visiting me in a couple of weeks. So just think about it, yeah? Come on, Caroline.' And off they went, to the sound of mysterious snorting, wheezing sounds from behind me.

I looked around at Cass and Alice. They were laughing so much I thought Cass was going to have some sort of fit. She was lying on the ground, gasping.

'Oh yes, it's all very funny,' I said. 'Me being used by a lunatic.'

'It is funny!' said Alice. 'Oh, come on, Bex. You know it is really.'

'It would be funny,' I said, 'if it were happening to someone else.'

'Oh my God,' wheezed Cass. 'I hope you're going to be in front of the tank ... riding the pony.' And she and Alice collapsed in hysterics again.

'Maybe she'll let us parade behind the tank like a marching band,' said Alice.

'Oooh yes,' said Cass. 'Please, Bex! Please let us march behind you and your new best friend!' And they both gazed at me with their hands clasped as if they were praying.

Oh, okay, it was a bit funny.

The maddest thing of all is that Vanessa really doesn't seem to believe that I'm not interested. We had a few classes together in the afternoon, and she kept smiling at me and giving me little waves. When I got home I told Mum all about it. At this stage I'm so used to telling her about the latest awful thing that has happened to me because of her stupid book that I don't even get angry about it. Well, only a little bit angry. When I'd stopped ranting and raving she said that Vanessa has a strong sense of self worth.

'A lot of teenage girls really hate themselves,' she said. 'But Vanessa seems to be very, um, confident. And confidence is healthy.'

'It's not that healthy,' I said. 'She's deluded.'

'Well, yes,' said Mum. 'She doesn't seem to be able to take no for an answer, anyway.' She paused. 'You know, I've said this before, but I really am sorry about all the fuss at school about Ruthie. I genuinely didn't think anything like this would happen.'

'Well, you should have,' I said. 'I could have told you it would be weird, if you'd bothered to tell me and Rachel about the book.'

'Yeah,' said Rachel, wandering in to the kitchen and grabbing an apple from the bowl on the counter. 'I can't believe you didn't realise how embarrassing this was going to be for us.'

'I know, and I'm sorry,' said Mum. 'But Vanessa's not that bad, is she? I mean, she's not bullying you or anything?'

'No one's bullying me,' I said. 'Even stupid Karen. They're just being annoying.'

Mum looked relieved. 'Well, that isn't good, but it's

not the end of the world either, right?'

'Huh,' I said. 'Easy for you to say.'

'Okay,' she said. 'Listen, I've learned over the last few weeks that it's better if I let you know in advance about anything to do with the new book. So I thought I should tell you that there's going to be an interview with me in a magazine that's out on Thursday. I'd have told you earlier, but I didn't know they were definitely going to run it until today. Don't worry,' she said, as Rachel and I opened our mouths to say something, 'there are no photos of you. In fact, I barely mentioned you at all. But bear in mind that I did the interview before the book came out so I didn't realise how upset you were going to be about being connected with it.'

Oh God. What does this mean? Please say she didn't use the word 'antics' again.

WEDNESDAY

I have been trying to avoid Vanessa since we discovered her nefarious plan, but that's easier said than done when you're in the same class. She keeps on trying to be nice to me and I've been ignoring her. And then today at lunch she lost her temper.

'Look,' she said. 'I don't see what the problem is. You get to help me be on telly, and then you get to go to my party. What's not good about that?'

'Vanessa,' I said, 'I dunno how to say this without sounding really rude ... but we're not actually friends. You've barely spoken to me for the last year. And now you're using me to try and get on telly. Why would I want to go to your party?'

'Because the party will be amazing and you'll get to be on 'My Big Birthday Bash', of course,' said Vanessa, in a way that suggested this was everyone's dream come true.

'It's not my sort of party,' I said, as if I'd been to loads of huge extravaganzas and knew exactly which ones I liked. 'Like I said, I don't want to be rude, but I'm not going to the party. I'm sure they'll let you on the programme anyway. Just tell them about the tank.'

'They know about that,' she said. 'It was in my application. I need something to surprise them.'

'Well, you're not getting me,' I said.

'Just think about it,' said Vanessa. And she went off before I could say anything else.

'That was kind of amazing,' said Cass. 'I wonder will she ever accept reality?'

'I think she's so used to her parents saying "yes" all the time that she actually doesn't understand when anyone says "no",' said Alice.

It truly is a wonder. I'm almost jealous of her. The world has got to be a nicer place if you actually don't notice anything negative. Although surely Vanessa can't keep this up forever. I mean, she's going to have to notice when she's having her birthday party and I'm not there.

Actually, who will be there? She doesn't really have any friends in school, apart from Caroline, not that that seems to bother her. She barely talks to anyone anyway. Maybe she has lots of rich friends none of us know about.

THURSDAY ☾

School was okay today. Karen Rodgers wasn't in, so there were no snide remarks about Wildfire, and Vanessa didn't do anything but give me meaningful looks and nods, as though we were members of the same secret cult. However, I am fairly sure that will all change as soon as someone in the class gets hold of the magazine that appeared today. I have now seen it and, although there are no photographs of me and Rachel, Mum says things like, 'I'd never have written this book if it weren't for my two girls,' and 'They're an inspiration to me – even if they don't know it.' There's also a huge photo of Mum sitting at a table covered in cakes in a fancy hotel, and I bet that will really convince Vanessa that Mum is rich and famous, which is the last thing I need.

FRIDAY ✯

Everyone knows about the gig! It was stupid Ellie's fault. I'm half tempted to tell everyone her name is really Galadriel. She deserves it. Our class was sitting around at lunchtime chatting in a big group (I was feeling quite nervous in case Karen Rodgers suddenly produced a copy of that magazine but no one seems to have seen it yet, thank GOD). Emma was telling us about the awful bridesmaid dress she's getting for her big sister's wedding.

'I can't even sit properly in it,' she said. 'It's like a cage. It's got metal bits in it to hold it up. And it's meant to, like, push my chest up, but there's not really enough to push so it just looks weird.'

'Speaking of weird dresses,' said Ellie, 'what are you three wearing to the Battle of the Bands next week?'

Cass, Alice and I all froze and stared at her.

'What battle of the bands?' said Jessie.

'Oops,' said Ellie, looking guilty. 'Sorry.'

'It's nothing,' said Cass.

'Yeah, we're not even sure whether we're doing it or not,' said Alice.

'Come on, tell us!' said Jessie. 'Are you playing a concert, then? Where is it on?'

And then everyone kept asking about it and in the end we cracked and told them it was next week. It's not like they wouldn't have been able to find out anyway. So now it seems like the entire class are going to be there. Including, of course, my number one fan, who emerged from behind the lockers when I was on my way to the first class after lunch.

'I can't wait for your concert,' said Vanessa.

'Thanks,' I said. 'Um, you know I'm still not going to your party, right?'

'We'll talk about that later,' she said, in a very grown-up way. 'I've got loads to do.'

As she turned to go, she took out her fancy phone and started to make a call.

'Hi, Robbie?' she said, sounding about thirty-five. 'Vanessa Finn here. Yeah, that's right.' Then she wandered off. I wish I could afford to make random phone calls during school hours, although now I come to think of it, who would I ring besides my parents? All my friends are in school too.

On the plus side, I did see Paperboy tonight. But only for a second. After last week's early visit I was on high alert practically from the moment I got home. I didn't even go upstairs for some drumming practice, even though I wanted to. And then, in the end, he just called at his usual time. I still feel all nervous and fluttery whenever I answer the door to him.

'Hey,' he said.

'Hey,' I said. I wish I could think of something amazing and funny to say to him every week. I try and think of things in advance, but nothing ever really comes to mind. Maybe there just aren't that many amazing, funny ways to greet someone who's just called to your house to collect newspaper money.

'So,' said Paperboy. 'Are you definitely going in for the Battle of the Bands?'

'Oh, yeah,' I said. 'Thanks for telling me about it.'

'No worries,' he said. 'Like I said, it should be a good laugh. Not that people will be laughing at you, obviously.'

'Well, I hope not,' I said.

'They might be laughing at Johnny's band, though,' said Paperboy. 'They've been, um, experimenting with hip hop recently. Results are mixed. Anyway, I hate to ask, but can I get some money from you?'

'Oh, sure,' I said, and ran back into the kitchen to get it. Mum gave me what I can only describe as a patronising grimace, but which I'm sure she thought was a wise smile.

'Paper money?' she said, holding out the coins. I took it off her and said nothing. I just glowered and stomped off. I've got very good at glowering at her in recent weeks.

Paperboy received his tribute.

'Thanks,' he said. 'And good luck! Your drumming

sounded great last week, by the way.'

And he strolled off before I could say anything.

I didn't bother ringing Alice or Cass to analyse everything. I just lay on my bed and thought about it. I wonder what I used to think about before I had Paperboy and the band to occupy me? I seem to think about them more than almost everything else these days. Well, apart from Mum's constant attempts to humiliate me. And global warming. And Vanessa.

Hmmm. I suppose I do think about a lot of things. But most of them seem to be kind of awful.

SATURDAY ★

Today we went shopping for clothes to wear on stage. Our parents have acknowledged that our very first gig is a special occasion and gave us each some cash, which sounds brilliant, except for the fact that we kept fighting over what to wear. Cass is still obsessed with our stage show.

'We need to look like a band,' she said when we met on Grafton Street.

'I think it's going to be fairly obvious we're a band,' said Alice. 'Seeing as we'll be standing on a stage holding instruments.'

'Or sitting behind them,' I reminded her.

Cass sighed. 'I mean we've got to have a look. A band look.'

'We're not wearing matching outfits, Cass,' I said. 'We'll just look like a terrible girl band then.'

'Yes, the last thing we need is Karen Rodgers calling us Wildfire,' said Alice.

'I don't mean matching outfits,' said Cass. 'I mean ... we've got to look like a team. Like, we can't just each wear something completely different.'

'Well, we wear quite similar clothes anyway,' said Alice, which is true. We do always like the same sort of things. 'Look, I think we should just wear clothes we like. We'll look cool then, but not as though we're trying too hard.'

This was true, of course, but the more I thought about it, though, the more I agreed with Cass. I did like the idea of us looking like a team. Or a gang.

'Why don't we all wear, say, dresses? Or all wear jeans and tops and Converse?' I said. 'That way we'll be linked, fashion-wise, but we won't all look the same.'

Everyone agreed to this inspired plan. But of course, then we had to decide what our common denominator, as they say in maths, was going to be. Cass thought dresses. Alice thought jeans. I should have been the casting vote, but I couldn't decide. We ended up practically shrieking at each other in the middle of Exchequer Street. Finally Cass said, 'Look, how many people do you think are going to be there in jeans? Probably all of them! If we're in dresses we'll stand out. And it's not like we don't wear dresses and skirts sometimes anyway.'

She had a point, as I said to Alice.

'I just don't want us to look as if we're trying too hard,' said Alice. 'Or being too girly.'

'There's nothing wrong with being girly, if you feel like it,' said Cass. 'We'll show them that girls can play instruments no matter what they're wearing.'

We all looked at each other.

'Okay,' said Alice. 'Dresses it is. But not, like, ball dresses or anything.'

'Oh, for goodness' sake,' said Cass. We spent the rest of the afternoon trying on frocks. In the end I got a red one with a white collar and buttons down the front, Cass got a navy one with red flowers, and Alice got a pale blue one with tiny cream dots all over. When our epic shop was over we went back to Cass's house and tried them on. We put on some make-up too. If we'd been in my house I could have begged Rachel to lend us some of hers. Nearly all her stuff is really posh, like Benefit and Nars and Laura Mercier, because she asks for it for her birthday. This is why she hides it away somewhere mysterious in her room so I can't get at it (although I still manage to steal – I mean borrow – some of it sometimes when she leaves it lying around the bathroom There is a blusher with a very rude name that makes me look all glowy. Sadly we didn't have any of that today but even our own stuff made us look pretty good. I used my mineral powder to stop my nose looking shiny and put on some smoky dark-grey eye-liner and pinky-nude lip gloss. Then we stood in front of the mirror in Cass's parents' room to see what we looked like all dressed up together. Unfortunately the mirror wasn't big enough for us to see each other at the same unless we went to the other side of the room, and then you couldn't see most of our legs because the bed was in the way.

'We can see enough,' said Cass. 'So ...'

'We look like a band,' said Alice. She took out her phone and took a photo of us. She has a posh phone that she got for her birthday and it's much better than the tiny little yokes me and Cass have. It's got a really good camera and the screen is nice and big so you can see photos on it properly. We all huddled around her and looked at it. Even on the little screen, we looked cooler than usual.

'Wow,' I said. 'We do look like a band.'

Because we did.

'Well, at least we don't clash with each other,' said Cass.

SUNDAY

Second last band practice before the big day. We're going to have a final one during the week.

'Maybe that should be our dress rehearsal,' said Cass, who really seems to think we're getting ready for some sort of huge superstar arena spectacular instead of an under-eighteens Battle of the Bands.

'Oh, come on,' said Alice. 'We don't need a dress

rehearsal. We're not wearing costumes and we don't have a set.'

'Maybe we should try playing in our new outfits,' said Cass. 'Just to get a feel for them.'

'You can wear yours if you like,' I said. 'But I'm saving mine until next Saturday. What if, I dunno, we spill something on them?'

'Like what?' said Cass.

'Well, I don't know! Tea! Or orange juice! Anything! Or I could trip over a lead and fall flat on my face and rip a hole in it.'

'I don't think that's very likely,' said Cass. 'It's never happened before.'

'It might,' I said. 'Why are you making such a fuss?'

'I just want to recreate what it'll be like on stage!' cried Cass.

'Well, we can't do that,' said Alice. 'Unless you also bring along a huge crowd, including half our class. Is that what you want to do?'

'Well, excuse me for actually caring about this stupid band!' said Cass. She looked as though she were about to burst into tears.

There was a pause.

'Um,' said Alice. 'I think we're all getting a bit ... worked up.' She looked around. Cass was leaning on her keyboard, and I was fiddling around with my drumsticks. None of us was looking directly at each other.

'I know we're all a bit stressed,' said Alice. 'But nothing's worth fighting over. Is it?'

'I suppose not,' mumbled Cass.

'Let's just play the Kinks' song again,' said Alice. 'Count us in, Bex.'

And I tapped my sticks together and cried, 'One, two, three, four!' and we all launched into the song. It's hard to feel stressed or cross when you're all bashing away at your instruments. I think we all felt a bit better when the song was over. The rest of the practice went fairly well. We made a few mistakes, but most of the time it sounds okay.

'You know,' said Cass, as we got into her mum's car, 'there's a chance we won't actually make fools of ourselves after all.'

I think she might actually be right.

MONDAY

How come every time something good happens – like us finding our stage outfits and having a good practice – something crap has to happen as well? Alice says this is the way of the universe and that we just have to accept the good and the bad in life, but I was not in the mood for her hippy wisdom today. As I feared, someone in school saw the magazine interview and now both Karen Rodgers and Vanessa are having a field day. Karen is the worst, of course. She says all these things like we're friends and she's having a hilarious joke but everyone knows that she's just being mean.

'I'm really looking forward to Wildfire's concert on Saturday,' she said. 'I see your mum's been talking to that magazine about what an inspiration you are, Rebecca. I knew she was just writing about your life.'

I ignored her, and so did Cass and Alice. But one person came to my defence. Unfortunately, it was Vanessa.

'You're just jealous,' she said to Karen. Which would

have been quite cool if she hadn't then said, 'I saw the photos of your mum, Rebecca. Your house is fabulous! I thought you lived in, like, one of those tiny little kips near Calderwood Road but I was obviously wrong. Amazing. And I loved the cakes. We're going to have loads of little cupcakes at the party, you know.'

'That wasn't our house,' I said. 'It was a hotel.'

'Oh,' said Vanessa.

'I actually do live in one of those tiny little kips near Calderwood Road,' I said.

'Oh, well, that doesn't matter,' said Vanessa. 'Your mum looked gorgeous, by the way.'

'Um, thanks,' I said.

'So what's the story with this concert thing you're doing on Saturday?' said Vanessa. 'Everyone's talking about it.'

'Oh, it's just a Battle of the Bands,' I said. 'For under-eighteens. It's not a big deal.'

'Oh please,' said Vanessa. 'It sounds fabulous. It's the Knitting Factory, right?'

'Right,' I said. 'But ...'

'Cool,' said Vanessa. 'Do you know what time you're playing at?'

'No,' I said. 'It starts at three o'clock, but we won't find out when we're on until we're there. But ...'

'Fabulous,' said Vanessa. 'Talk soon, yeah?'

And she was gone.

'She really is a very strange girl,' said Cass. 'I wonder will she actually turn up on Saturday?'

'Well, it seems as though everyone else will,' I said. 'I bet they're going to have a great laugh.'

'Oh, don't be silly,' said Alice. 'I know you're feeling a bit paranoid at the moment, but you do realise people are actually coming to cheer us on, right?'

'Karen isn't,' I said.

'Oh, who cares about Karen?' said Alice. 'She's just snotty to everyone and no one really likes her. But most people like you.'

'Or at least they don't dislike you,' said Cass.

'Thanks, Cass,' I said.

'Well, anyway, people are coming because they like all of us,' said Alice. 'More or less. And they want to see the band.'

Which is definitely better than people coming along to laugh at us. Although it also puts us under pressure. But that's probably good for us. I have to admit that I POSSIBLY wouldn't have practised the drums so much recently if it weren't for the Battle of the Bands. The Battle gave me something to aim for. And now I can actually play them. Well, kind of. No, I can really.

TUESDAY

Because I can't stop thinking about band stuff, I am finding it very hard to concentrate in school. Mrs O'Reilly (no relation to my fictional nemesis Ruthie) was asking me a question about some old explorer for about ten minutes today and I didn't hear her because I was staring at the window, wondering whether I should wear tights with my gig dress or risk bare legs.

'I don't know what's got into you, Miss Rafferty,' she said. 'You're worse than ever recently.'

I couldn't argue (not that she'd have listened if I had) because alas it is true. It's not as though I'm an incredibly hard worker at the best of times, but I really have been a bit slack about doing actual studying over the last few weeks.

Still, how can I be expected to concentrate on ancient explorers and German verbs when I have to go on stage and play the drums in front of hundreds of strangers AND my entire class in just four days?

And as if I wasn't thinking about the gig too much anyway, Mrs Harrington has somehow heard about the Battle of the Bands (HOW? Surely Karen can't have told her? Maybe she really is spying on Mum and by extension the entire family) and now she keeps making 'hilarious' comments about it.

'Now we know where your mammy got her inspiration for Wildfire!' she said with a simper.

'Well, we're a very different sort of band,' I said. 'We play our own instruments and we write our own songs.' Which isn't totally a lie. We wrote one of our songs. And we only have two.

But Mrs Harrington didn't seem to hear me.

'I hope there's no rivalry in the band, though,' she said. 'Remember what happened to Ruthie and Wildfire!'

How could I ever forget? They are hanging over me at all times. I never thought I'd miss those awful Irish dancing kids, but I do now.

WEDNESDAY ✿

My parents have announced that they want to come to the Battle of the Bands. Of course, there is no way I will let this happen.

'Oh, come on, Bex,' said my dad. 'It's our baby daughter's first gig! Of course we want to be there.'

'You can't come,' I cried. 'You'll be the oldest people by about fifty years.'

'Well, I don't think that's true,' said Dad, 'considering I'm only thirty-two years older than you.'

'You know what I mean,' I said. 'Anyway, the fact that you just referred to me as your "baby daughter" shows that you shouldn't be allowed in. You'll disgrace me! Again. And it's not like you haven't been doing that a lot recently.'

'But we want to cheer you on,' said Mum. She looked quite sad.

'Mum,' I said. 'I appreciate your support, but all of my class will be there, and they've been slagging me off about you quite enough recently. So the last thing I need is you turning up in person.'

'They won't know we're your parents,' said Mum. 'We could be anyone's parents. I bet we won't be the only ones, too.'

'First of all, I'm sure everyone else's parents will be sensible enough not to come, and second of all, everyone in school knows what you look like because you've been all over the papers, as well as eating cakes in silly magazines.'

'Oh,' said Mum. She sighed. 'Well, I suppose you're right. Oh well.'

I felt a bit bad. 'You know this won't be your only chance to see us ever,' I said. At least, I hope it won't. 'There'll be plenty of gigs. So you'll get to see us eventually.'

Mum and Dad sort of grinned at each other.

'Okay,' said Mum. 'We won't embarrass you for now. Would you and the girls like a lift to the venue anyway?'

'Oooh, yes please,' I said. Mum still does have her uses. I suppose she's not that bad really.

THURSDAY ☾

Last practice before the battle of the bands. We don't sound too bad. Actually, when we get through a song without a mistake, we sound pretty good. The only problem is that this doesn't happen every time we play the songs. But it happens more often than it doesn't. And I've got better at looking out at the (imaginary, for now) audience while I play. We went through both songs about a million times. My voice was hoarse after a while, but luckily Alice's mother is being extremely kind (she really is much nicer than Mum) and brought us out some soothing honey and lemon drinks that she'd made herself.

'The singing sounds okay,' said Alice. She's right, actually. The three of us singing together sounds pretty cool. It makes the Kinks' song sound brand new and our own song actually sounds ... kind of good.

I'm scared to be too optimistic about the whole thing in case I jinx it, but every so often I allow myself to imagine what it MIGHT be like. Like, I imagine us all up on the stage, looking really cool and confident, and playing the songs perfectly, and the audience going wild. Of course, in my imagination I don't need to look at my drums all the time so I can gaze out confidently at the audience. I also look very elegant and have perfect hair, and I have the ability to throw my drumsticks into the air and catch them again, without missing a beat. That's possibly the most unrealistic bit. I have no idea how proper drummers do it, because, every time I try, I can't catch either of the sticks at all, let alone without missing a beat. I've stopped trying now, because the last time I tried one of the drumsticks nearly poked me in the eye as it fell. I'm not risking blindness just to do a cool drumstick trick.

FRIDAY ☆

Feeling very, very nervous about tomorrow. I couldn't concentrate in any class today. I really wish no one at school knew about it. It seems like the entire class is going to turn up. Even Karen Rodgers, for some freakish reason.

'I can't wait to see you and Wildfire tomorrow,' she said

at lunch. 'We all need a few laughs, don't we?'

I ignored her, which shows how grown-up I have become as a result of all my suffering. Well, I didn't say anything, at least. I just made a face at her.

Cass is trying to look on the bright side of everyone coming to the battle of the bands. 'Well, at least if we're brilliant everyone will see us,' she said. 'That should stop people going on about your mum's book all the time.'

'Aren't you nervous?' said Alice. 'Because I certainly am. Every time I think about the gig being on being tomorrow I get a weird churning feeling in my tummy. It's awful.'

'Me too,' I said. 'Don't you, Cass?'

'I dunno,' said Cass. 'It's stopped seeming so scary now. I mean, we're not brilliant, but it's not like we're going to, I dunno, fall off the stage or anything.'

Alice and I just looked at each other.

'Are you sure you're all right, Cass?' said Alice. 'I mean, you seem strangely calm.'

Cass looked faintly surprised. 'Yeah, I suppose I am. I mean, I'm excited and everything. But now it's actually happening, I'm not really that scared.'

Somehow seeing Cass in such a weirdly serene mood made me and Alice feel a bit more calm too. Although I hope Cass's calmness today doesn't mean she's going to totally freak out tomorrow. Maybe she's going to be all calm and sensible until we're actually on stage and then she's going to wet herself or something. Oh God.

Okay, I'm feeling even more nervous now. And this feeling isn't helped by the fact that Paperboy is definitely going to be there tomorrow. I nearly broke my neck this evening running out to answer the door when he called for his paper money. Rachel pretended that she was running out too but she was only doing it to make me run faster. I could hear her laughing like a loon when I opened the door.

'Hi!' I said.

Paperboy looked a bit startled, probably because I'd just flung the door open like I was trying to escape from a serial killer.

'Hey,' he said. 'Looking forward to setting the world on fire with your amazing drumming?'

'Sort of,' I said. 'You know, there's actually a chance we will literally set something on fire. We're all very nervous.

We'll probably pull down a light or something.'

'Ah, don't worry about it,' said Paperboy. 'You'll be grand. Everyone's nervous anyway. My friend Johnny keeps saying he doesn't think he can do it at all.'

'No, really?' I said, very relieved. It felt much better to know that we weren't the only people freaking out.

'Yes, he keeps having nightmares where he gets on stage and discovers they've left all their instruments at home so they have to do a ridiculous dance routine instead.'

'Hmmm,' I said. 'Well, there's no way we're doing a dance routine, even if we do leave everything at home. That's just what a stupid girl in my class wants me to do.'

Paperboy looked confused. 'Why? Is she a fan of your dancing?'

I wished I hadn't said anything now, but I had to explain about Ruthie's awful group.

'So you see, there will be no dancing from me,' I said. 'Karen Rodgers would have a field day. I'd never hear the end of it.'

'Fair enough,' said Paperboy. 'Anyway, I'm sure you won't forget anything.'

'I don't even have to bring my drums,' I said. 'They're

giving us a kit. I mean, they're giving all the bands the same kit. I just have to bring my drumsticks.'

'Well, if you do manage to forget them – and Johnny's drummer remembers his – I'm sure I can get a loan of them for you.'

'Oh, thanks. So ...' I said. I've been so nervous about the battle that I'd forgotten to be nervous about Paperboy. Apparently I can't really be nervous about two things at once. Hmmm. 'So are you going, then?'

'But of course!' said Paperboy. 'I'm making banners and flags and t-shirts and everything.'

'Really?' I said.

'Um, no,' said Paperboy. 'Sorry. But I'll be cheering.'

He smiled at me. And I smiled back. I hope I didn't look too weird. I caught sight of myself smiling in the hall mirror the other day when I was on the phone to Cass and I looked a bit deranged. When I got off the phone I practised smiling in the mirror for a bit to see if there was a way I could smile and still look nice, but I just looked madder and madder. Magazines are always saying everyone looks better when they smile, but I don't think this is true in my case. I don't think I have a very symmetrical face.

Anyway, I had to stop smiling at Paperboy (which was probably for the best, given my peculiar face) because my dad called out from the kitchen, 'Rebecca? Is that the paperboy? Do you need the money?'

'Yes!' I shouted back. 'Um, back in a second.' And then I had to run into the kitchen because otherwise Dad would have come out to give me the paper money. If he did, he'd probably have started asking me and Paperboy what we were talking about and making some 'hilarious' dad-esque jokes, to show how cool and hip he is. My parents have embarrassed me enough recently, so I'm not going to hand either of them any more opportunities.

When I gave the money to Paperboy I said, 'So, I'll see you tomorrow?'

And he said, 'You definitely will. I'm looking forward to it. Good luck!'

And off he went. I immediately ran to phone Cass to analyse his words.

'Do you think he's looking forward to seeing us or just the whole thing?' I said.

'He must be looking forward to seeing us a little bit,' said Cass. 'Or why would he have said it at all?'

'I do really like him, you know,' I said. I paused. 'Do you ...?'

Because at the beginning Cass seemed to like him as well. She hasn't seen him since, but that doesn't necessarily make a difference. I would feel weird if we both felt the same way about him. But it looks like we actually don't.

'Nah,' said Cass. 'Seriously, I don't. I mean, he is extremely good looking and everything. But when you told me about his girlfriend ...'

'Ex-girlfriend,' I said quickly.

'Yes, ex-girlfriend,' said Cass. 'I didn't really feel anything. I mean, it made you feel sick and horrible, but not me. So I don't think he is the love of my life or anything.'

I felt very relieved. I wouldn't want any boys to come between me and Cass, and not just because that would make us like Ruthie and her so-called friends. But because even though I don't know whether Paperboy likes me at all, and he probably doesn't (although sometimes I really think he might), I would hate for Cass and me to be rivals. It would be wrong. Her and me and Alice are a team, and not just because we're in a band. Although that does make us feel even more team-ish.

Anyway, both Cass and I are going to try and have an early night. We have to be fresh-faced and beautiful for our debut tomorrow. Well, fresh-faced anyway.

LATER

I can't sleep! I have been lying awake thinking of everything that could go wrong tomorrow. To distract myself, I will try imagining what it would be like if we were interviewed for one of the fancy music magazines Dad buys.

It's hard to believe it's only a few weeks since Dublin trio Hey Dollface got together in their north Dublin studio. Rebecca Rafferty, Cassandra McDermott and Alice Sheridan play like seasoned professionals.

In an elegant and supercool dress, Rafferty radiates star quality, her glossy, bouncy hair shining as she keeps perfect time. Her skilful and complicated drumming puts older musicians to shame. 'I suppose I just have natural rhythm,' says the beautiful drummer, tossing her drumsticks into the air mid-beat.

Surely it is only a matter of time before such things appear in magazines for real?

Okay, I'm actually starting to feel tired now. Let's hope I actually get some sleep. This time tomorrow it'll all be over ...

SATURDAY ★

Today was ... well, it was one of the strangest, most amazing days of my life. I'd better start at the beginning. Which I suppose is this morning, which I spent wandering aimlessly around the house or fiddling with my drumsticks because I couldn't concentrate on anything else. This perfectly innocent behaviour was, of course, too much for Rachel.

'Oh my God, will you just sit down?' she said. 'You're doing my head in, roaming around like a mad ghost.'

'I'm too stressed to sit down,' I said. 'Alice's mum is dropping her here and then we're going to get Cass. So I have nothing to do but wait for them.'

Rachel sighed. 'Okay,' she said. 'How about we go over your stage ensemble? And your make-up? You've got to leave in half an hour, you know. It's getting late. You've been wandering around all morning.'

'I don't want to wear loads of make-up,' I said. 'I might look like Ruthie. Or Vanessa. Anyway, I never wear loads of make-up.' I paused. 'I don't even own loads of make-up.'

'Don't worry,' said Rachel. 'I'm not going to make you look like a clown.' She grinned evilly. 'Or am I?'

'Oh, go away,' I said. 'I'm nervous enough without you making fun of me. You're not funny.'

'Oh, come on,' said Rachel. 'I'm only joking. Go on, show me your dress again.'

So I went upstairs and tried it on. Rachel looked very serious. 'Hmmm, very nice,' she said. 'No, seriously, it is. Go for the tights, though, not bare legs. As for your hair ...'

She hovered over me for a while, doing painful things with a brush, some clips, and her anti-frizz serum stuff. Finally she sighed.

'I'm afraid your hair is always going to be a bit odd,' she said. 'But this isn't too bad.'

I looked in the mirror. It was a bit unruly, because it always is, but it did look much glossier and neater than usual.

'Ooh, thanks,' I said.

'Now for your make-up,' declared Rachel.

She made me close my eyes while she got out her make-up bag so I wouldn't see her secret hiding place and messed around with some eye-liner, creamy Benefit eye-shadow in a smoky sort of shade called Skinny Jeans and this really posh mascara that's meant to make you look like you're wearing false eyelashes. Every so often I said, 'Ow!' and 'Don't poke me in the eye!'

Finally, she stopped poking me and looked at me thoughtfully. 'Hmmm,' she said. 'Not bad. It'll have to do, anyway. Just don't cry or rub your eyes, you'll wreck it.'

'I hope I don't have any reason to cry,' I said nervously. Then I looked in the mirror. And I have to admit, Rachel had done a pretty good job. My eyes looked huge and my lashes looked about an inch long.

'You just need some nude lip gloss with that,' said Rachel. She sighed. 'I suppose you could borrow this Laura Mercier one ...'

'Thanks, Rachel,' I said.

'Don't worry about it,' she said. 'Our family all have to look our best in the public eye at the moment to make up for Mum's madness.'

'Rebecca!' called Mum from downstairs. 'Alice is here! Are you ready? We'd better go!'

'I'll see you in there later,' said Rachel. 'Break a leg!'

And I was off. Alice had brought the guitar and the keyboard and she looked lovely. Her hair was at its most German and she looked all peachy and glowy.

'Imagine if we were this glamorous all the time,' I said.

'It's too much work, really,' said Alice. 'We'd never have time for band practice if we spent all our time dressing up and putting on perfect make-up.'

'True,' I said. We had reached Cass's house and I ran out to get her. Her little brother Nick answered the door.

'Is Cass there?' I said.

'No,' said Nick.

'What?' I shrieked. Had Cass had an attack of nerves and run away? I knew she was eerily calm this week ...

'She's been kidnapped by aliens,' said Nick. 'And they've left some stranger with loads of make-up.'

'Oh, shut up, Nick,' said Cass. She looked lovely and she wasn't wearing lots of make-up at all. I suppose just a bit of eye shadow and blusher looks like a lot to Nick. Cass hardly wears any eye-make-up usually because of the whole glasses thing (she thinks you can't see it behind the specs, but you can and it still looks nice) and I don't think their mum even owns mascara. Speaking of Cass's mum, she came out to wish us good luck.

'I'm very proud of you all,' she said. 'I wish you'd let me and your dad go, Cass.'

'Next time,' said Cass. 'Come on, Bex, we'd better go.'

We said goodbye to Cass's mum, ignored Nick, and headed to the car.

'Right,' said Mum. 'Before we leave this part of town – do you have everything you need? Instruments, drum-sticks?'

We did.

'Right,' said Mum. 'We're off.'

'Are you sure you want to do this?' I said loftily. 'I don't want you to feel bad about actually doing something to improve my life. For once.'

Mum rolled her eyes and drove on.

In what seemed like about two seconds, we were in town. Mum dropped us off outside the venue.

'Good luck, girls,' she said. 'Are you absolutely and

totally sure you don't want me and your dad to come along later?'

'Yes!' I cried. 'But, um, thanks very much for the lift.'

'No problem,' she said. 'I'll see you out here at six, okay? Give me or your dad a ring if there are any problems.'

So there we were, at our first gig. We each looked at each other, took a deep breath, and headed inside. Cass and I carried her keyboard between us. A young man was standing inside the door checking off names on a list.

'Which band are you?' he said.

'Hey Dollface,' said Alice.

The man grinned and ticked something on his list. 'Cool name. There's just three of you, right?'

We nodded.

'Great. Okay, best of luck!'

There was a big crowd inside the venue – there were probably about sixty or seventy people there. It was mostly boys.

'Wow,' whispered Alice, a bit nervously. 'I don't think I've ever been in a place where there were so many boys and hardly any girls.'

'I have,' said Cass. 'When my parents make me go to my stupid brother's football matches.' She paused. 'Though of course they're all about ten so it doesn't really count.'

Everyone was just shuffling around, looking slightly unsure of themselves. Lots of people had taken their guitars out of their cases and were strumming at them quietly. We weren't the only girls, though, which was cool – there were a couple of girls about our age holding guitars and basses and a few without instruments who turned out to be singers. We were in the minority though. I think that's why we all ended up catching each other's eyes and kind of smiling at each other in the crowd.

Suddenly Alice said, 'Oh my God!'

Cass and I both said, 'What?' really loudly.

'Ssssh,' hissed Alice. 'You will never guess who's here. Over there. No, don't point! To the right, near the bar.'

Cass and I both looked and then gasped.

'It's Bike Boy!' I said.

'Ssssh!' said Alice.

'Oh, come on,' I said. 'He's on the other side of the room and it's very noisy. He's not going to hear me.'

'He might notice us and realise that we're talking about

him,' said Alice. 'I can't believe he's here.'

'He's got a bass,' said Cass. 'Oooh, he's looking over here!'

'Stop staring!' said Alice.

'I think he's seen us,' I said.

'Shut up!' said Alice, edging behind me.

'Alice, if you don't want him to notice you, maybe you should stop acting so weirdly,' said Cass. 'That hissing and skulking isn't very inconspicuous.'

Then a woman came on to the stage with a clipboard. She was quite old, about thirty I think, but she was wearing cool clothes and seemed very nice and friendly. She grabbed a microphone from a stand.

'Hey everyone,' she said. 'Welcome to the Battle of the Bands! I'm Veronica, one of the organisers, and I'll be doing the sound for you this afternoon. I know that for a lot of you this is your first gig, so lots of luck – I know you'll all be brilliant. Now, we just about have time for everyone to do a very short soundcheck – like, half a song – just to make sure we can hear you out here and you can all hear yourselves on stage. If there's anything that doesn't sound right when you're doing your soundcheck, just say something and we'll change it. We've got a fairly basic set-up – most of you are just using one or two microphones, but from the details you gave us when you registered, we know that a few of you need three. So we'll check you lot first.' Cass, Alice and I looked at each other in horror. We need three microphones! 'When I call the name of your band, come up to the stage.' She looked down at her notes. 'Okay ... first up, it's The Retreat.'

Four skinny boys made their way up the stairs at the side of the stage. They didn't look very happy about being the first band to play anything. I didn't blame them – I was just glad it wasn't us. The stage was full of amplifiers and, in the middle, the drum kit. It was on a platform towards the rear of the stage, looking huge and impressive. The boys in The Retreat said a few words to Veronica, and then she and the bloke who had been ticking off names at the door moved some of the microphone stands around. Veronica jumped off the stage and went over to the mixing desk at the back of the venue.

'Okay, boys!' she said. 'Let's hear you.'

'What'll we do if they're amazingly brilliant?' whispered Cass.

'Run away,' said Alice.

The band started playing. And to my relief, they weren't amazingly brilliant. They weren't terrible either, though. They were fairly good. Not that we got a chance to hear much of them. They played for about a minute and then Veronica's voice rang out over the speakers.

'That's great, lads,' she said. 'How does it sound to you? Can you hear your vocals in the monitors?'

One of the boys said he could do with it being a bit louder, so Veronica did some fiddling around on her mixing desk and asked them to try again. They played a few bars and said it was okay.

'Great,' said Veronica. 'Thanks, everyone. Now, next up it's ... Hey Dollface.'

The walk to the stage seemed to take about five years, not least because I was helping Cass carry the keyboard which suddenly felt about five times heavier than usual. I couldn't help glancing over in Bike Boy's direction to see if he'd seen us. He had, and looked surprised. We clambered up the stairs and tried to pretend there weren't loads of people staring at us as we set the keyboard on its stand. The bloke from the door walked over and smiled.

'Hey, I'm Paul,' he said. 'So you each need a mike, right? '

We nodded. I think we were all too scared to speak.

'Okay,' said Paul. 'Which of you is the drummer?'

'Me,' I said, in a tiny little voice.

'Right,' said Paul. 'You sit yourself down behind the drums and I'll get the mike ready for you.'

So I climbed onto the drum platform. It felt very exposed. I'd been kind of relieved at the idea that I could hide away at the back of the stage. But I hadn't realised the platform was so high. I felt like everyone was staring at me. Which some of them probably were. Paul moved some mikes around and adjusted the heights of the stands.

'Right,' he said. 'That should be fine. Okay, off you go!'

'What song will we do?' whispered Alice, as she tuned her guitar. She looked terrified.

'The Kinks one,' said Cass. 'It's easier.'

We all nodded at each other. I was so nervous I was worried my hands were going to start shaking. Then I banged the sticks together and shouted, 'One, two, three, four!' And then I hit the tom drum.

It didn't sound brilliant, but it sounded okay. At first it

felt weird playing a strange drum kit AND singing into a microphone, but it didn't make too much of a difference. When we all started singing, I was worried that I wouldn't be able to hear the others' voices, but I could hear Alice singing perfectly. I wasn't sure I could hear Cass at all, though. After what seemed like a split second, Veronica interrupted us.

'That sounds good, girls,' she said. 'Can you hear yourselves okay?'

I hated the idea of speaking into the microphone in front of all those people, but I knew I needed to make sure I could hear properly.

'Um, could I hear more of Cass's singing? I mean the keyboard player.'

'And can I hear more of Rebecca's voice?' said Alice. 'She's the drummer.'

'Sure,' said Veronica. She did something to the desk. 'Okay, try it again.'

We did, and sure enough I could now hear both Alice and Cass singing perfectly. She didn't sound half bad.

'Is that okay?' said Veronica. We looked at each other and nodded again. Maybe we are developing a psychic link with each other. Eventually we won't have to speak at all.

'It's fine,' said Cass.

'Great,' said Veronica. 'Okaaay ... next up, it's The Tools.'

We gathered up our stuff and got off the stage as quickly as we could.

'That wasn't so bad,' said Cass.

'I suppose not,' said Alice. 'But just think what it'll be like when we're doing entire songs in front of a crowd. Including people we know.'

'Including Paperboy,' I said, feeling a bit sick.

'Including Bike Boy too,' said Cass.

'Where, where?' said Alice.

'He's still over near the bar,' I said. 'Oh, I think he's looking at us. He is!'

'Quick, let's find somewhere to sit down,' said Alice.

'Oooh, Alice, you're bright red,' said Cass.

'Shut up,' said Alice, scuttling off. We sat down at a table at the side of the hall. The next band weren't very good. They were another all-boy four piece and the lead singer was strutting around the stage in a really cocky way, like he was headlining a huge festival, instead of just checking the sound at a small gig. I hoped they weren't Paperboy's mates. Then there was a duo who were kind of folksy and a bit boring. After them came a band called Bad Monkey, with three girls and a boy drummer. The girls looked really cool, especially the lead singer. She had a lovely turquoise electric guitar and a great choppy short haircut. They were really good too, much better than the other bands we'd seen so far (including ourselves).

'That's it, we're not winning tonight,' said Cass. 'They're the coolest people here.'

'Stop that, Cass,' said Alice. 'We'll be great.'

We sat there for ages, watching the other bands play snatches of songs. It was really boring, to be honest. Apparently being in a band is not always fun and exciting. It also involves just hanging around big stuffy rooms while other people do things.

'Some people are going out of the venue for a while,' I said, indicating the boys from The Retreat who were heading out the front door. Another of the bands who'd played earlier was just coming in clutching sandwiches and cans of Coke. 'Let's go out and get some fresh air. And maybe some chocolate. We've got half an hour before the concert starts, so we've got loads of time.'

'You go,' said Alice. 'I'll wait here and guard our stuff.'

'Are you sure?' said Cass.

Alice said she was, so Cass and I grabbed our jackets and headed outside. We passed Bike Boy on the way and he raised his hand in greeting. I sort of waved back, and then turned to Cass.

'That's why she doesn't want to leave,' I said. 'Bike Boy! His band haven't played yet.'

'So they haven't,' said Cass. 'Hmmm. What do you think? I'd quite like to see what they're like, but I really want a Dairy Milk.'

'We'll see what they're like later,' I said. 'Come on, let's go.'

It was nice to get out of the dark, stuffy Knitting Factory. We got some sandwiches and chocolate and strolled lazily in the sun back towards the venue.

'Did you ever think, when this term started, that just a few months later we'd be getting ready for our first gig?' said Cass.

'I really didn't,' I said. I threw my bag of sandwiches into the air and caught it again.

'You know, I'm sorry about being so unenthusiastic when we were starting the band,' said Cass. 'I was just worried that we'd be crap and it would just be depressing. But we're not.'

'And even if we were a bit crap,' I said, 'which we're not, of course, I think it would still be fun. Wouldn't it?'

'Yeah, probably,' said Cass. 'Come on, we'd better go back. I don't think Alice wants to sit there gazing at Bike Boy on her own for too long.'

So we hurried back into the venue. As soon as we walked into the main part of the venue, we looked at the stage and there was Bike Boy, playing a bass and singing in a rather dramatic and gloomy fashion. We made our way through the crowd to Alice, who was looking at the stage with a strange expression on her face.

'Are you okay?' I said. 'We got you a sandwich.'

'Are you looking at him with love or are you wondering why he's making those weird faces?' said Cass. 'And singing in that peculiar booming voice?'

'Hmm,' said Alice. 'A bit of both. Maybe. What sandwich did you get me?'

'Egg and bacon,' I said. 'What's his band like?' Because

Bike Boy had stopped playing the bass and singing in a deep voice and had said, 'Thanks very much,' to Veronica in his normal one. His band's soundcheck was over.

'They're quite good, actually,' said Alice. 'But ... well, it's like he's in a play. He sings as though he was acting a character. It's quite cool, though, I think. And he's wearing a great suit!'

We all looked at Bike Boy with confusion. He did look quite good in the suit. But how did a boy our age have a suit like that?

'Hey,' said an unfamiliar voice. We looked around and the lead singer of Bad Monkey was smiling at us in a shy way. 'Just wanted to say it's nice to see some more girls in the competition. We entered last year and we were the only ones! You sounded good, too.'

'So did you,' said Cass.

The girl's name was Liz and she told us she and the rest of the band went to school together at a mixed school on the southside. She was very nice and said that at last year's Battle of the Bands they were all so scared that the bass player, Katie, threw up just before they went on stage.

'In the toilet, though,' she added. 'Not, like, on the steps.'

Liz was lovely. She stayed chatting with us for a few minutes (we told her that we'd only been together for just over a month and she seemed pretty impressed) until we heard someone call her name. It was Katie, the pukey bassist. 'Sorry to interrupt,' she called. 'But we need to check a few things.'

'Coming!' said Liz. She turned back to us. 'Best of luck!'

'Same to you,' I said. And off she went to her band. One of them was holding up a guitar and looking worried. I heard her say 'It just won't stay in tune ...'

'Well, if we win I hope they come second,' said Cass.

'I think it'll be the other way round,' I said. 'If we're lucky.'

The last band (they weren't bad apart from when the lead singer did a very bad rap in the middle that didn't really go with the rest of the song) finished their soundcheck and Veronica got up on the stage.

'Okay, everyone,' she said. 'You all sound great, and you've been very patient. Now, we're going to open the doors in a minute, but before we do, I just need to tell you that we've printed out the running order so you can see when you're going to be on stage – it's over there at the sound desk. It's basically in reverse order to the sound-check, so if you soundchecked first, you'll perform last, and the other way around. And the first band – that's you, Flash Harry – will be on in about twenty minutes. Okay? Best of luck, everyone!'

'Eeek,' said Cass. 'This is it.'

The lights in the main part of the hall dimmed slightly and the lights on the stage got brighter. Even though none of the audience had arrived yet, the atmosphere changed. Everyone looked a bit jittery. The bar opened – it wasn't selling any alcohol, of course – and people started hanging around it, shakily knocking back soft drinks. I saw one boy surreptitiously take a can of beer out of his bag as the first few members of the audience trickled into the hall.

Cass and Alice and I just sort of hovered around near our stuff as more and more people came through the doors.

'Oh God, it's starting to fill up,' said Alice.

'Ugh, I just wish it would start,' said Cass. 'I hate this hanging around.'

'Me too,' I said. Then I saw some familiar faces in the crowd near the door. 'Hey, look – it's Ellie and Emma!' I waved furiously and they came over.

'Wow, look at you!' said Emma. 'You all look very rock and roll.'

'I don't know if I feel it,' said Cass.

'Well, as long as we can act it, that's all that counts,' said Alice. What has got into her lately? She is a fount of wisdom. Then she froze. 'Bex, don't look around, but Vanessa just walked in. Maybe if we don't move, she won't see us.'

But it was too late.

'Rebecca, hi!' shrieked Vanessa. I risked a glance in the direction of the shriek and saw that she was heading straight towards us with what I could only describe as an entourage. She was, of course, accompanied by Caroline, her faithful sidekick, but she also had two adults who looked like they were in their thirties. They also looked, as Cass said later, 'haunted. Like they'd witnessed something horrible and unmentionable.'

'Oh my God,' whispered Cass. 'Who is that old man? Can he be her boyfriend?'

'Surely not,' I said. 'We'd have heard all about that.' By now Vanessa was upon us. She was wearing a tiny little dress which looked like it had been painted on, and a pair of heels so high I'm amazed she could walk so fast. Quite a contrast to her usual fluffy boots. She was also wearing more make-up than me, Cass and Alice put together.

'How are you?' she cried, grabbing me and planting air kisses in the general direction of each of my cheeks.

'I'm fine,' I said. 'I have to get on a stage and play some songs soon, though, so ...'

But Vanessa, as usual, wasn't listening.

'Robbie, Sarah, this is my friend Rebecca, the girl I was telling you about,' she said.

The man, Robbie, extended a hand. I shook it. 'Hi, Rebecca, good to meet you,' he said. He had an English accent.

'Hi,' I said. 'Um, I think I should tell you ...'

'This is Sarah,' said Vanessa, shoving the woman in my direction.

'Hi, Rebecca, Vanessa has told us all about you,' said Sarah with a tired smile. 'She says your mother is the author Rosie Carberry, is that true?'

'Well, yes,' I said. 'but ...'

'Yeah, I read about her new teen book. That's great, that's doing really well. She's a big name in teen fiction now. And how long have you and Vanessa been friends?'

'We've been in the same class since we started secondary school last year,' I said. 'But to be honest ...'

Vanessa butted in. 'I don't know what I'd do without Becca,' she said. 'We're like sisters, aren't we, Becca?'

'Becca?' said Cass.

'And this is Becca's band,' Vanessa went on. 'They're all going to play at my party.'

'Of course,' said Robbie. 'We can't wait to see you. It sounds like you're going to be the highlight of Vanessa's big birthday bash.'

Cass, Alice and I looked at each other in wonder.

'You're from the TV show?' said Alice.

'Yes, we're the researchers,' said Sarah. 'Didn't Vanessa tell you? We're over for the weekend, to interview her about her party. It sounds like it'll be ... spectacular.'

'It certainly does,' said Cass.

'I've just ordered a pink crane,' said Vanessa proudly. 'I'm going to be lowered into the marquee on a throne.'

Robbie looked at Sarah. 'I think I need a drink,' he said. 'Do you need a drink?'

'Yes,' said Sarah fervently. 'Come on Vanessa, Caroline

– we'll get you a coke. Good luck, girls.'

'See you later, Becca!' said Vanessa, and they all marched off. The rest of us just stared at each other.

'I don't believe it,' I said. 'I don't believe after everything I said, she's actually told a TV company that I'm her best mate and that we're going to play at her ridiculous party.'

'Wow, she really can't accept reality, can she?' said Ellie. 'And neither can those TV people if they think they're going to get any alcohol at that bar.' She looked around. 'Oh, hi, Rebecca's sister.'

'Hello, Rebecca's friend,' said Rachel. She had arrived with her friend Jenny, who gave us a friendly smile. 'Who on earth was that girl?'

'That was Vanessa Finn,' I said wearily.

'Oh, the mad one,' said Rachel. 'Right, what time are you on?'

'Second last,' said Cass.

'Okay,' said Rachel. 'So Jenny and I have time to go off and get a drink somewhere.'

'I suppose so,' I said.

'Don't worry, we're not going to miss you,' she said. 'We'll be back in half an hour.'

'We definitely will,' said Jenny. 'It's just the thought of sitting through loads of kids – I mean, other bands. See you later!'

And off they ponced. I stared after them.

'Oh well, she's here in spirit,' said Cass. 'And you know she'll come back in time to see us.'

'Yeah, I know,' I said. And I did. She wouldn't have bothered turning up at all if she wasn't going to see us play. 'I'm just jealous because she can escape for a while.'

'Oh, look, some more of the class are here,' said Alice. 'Oh my God, it looks like all of our class is here.'

And sure enough, a big gang of our classmates had just come through the door. I saw Anne O'Hara and Jessie and – oh yes – Karen Rodgers. And almost everyone else.

'Why on earth is Karen here?' I said. 'She doesn't even like me!'

'She's just looking for ammunition,' sighed Cass.

'Wow,' said Alice. 'I didn't think so many would turn up. They're all coming this way.'

Suddenly I couldn't bear the thought of having to talk to loads of people at once.

'I'm going to the loo,' I said, and ran off. Luckily the

bathrooms were in the opposite direction to the entrance. Once I was in there I sat in a stall and tried to do the deep breathing exercises Ellie taught us last year (her mum is very into deep-breathing exercises, unsurprisingly). When I felt a bit better I headed out, and I was half way across the hall when someone said, 'Hey,' and tapped my shoulder. I turned around and there was Paperboy, looking gorgeous. And tall. Oh, he's so tall.

'Hey,' I said. I hoped I didn't look as awe-struck as I felt.

'You look – are you all set for the gig?' said Paperboy.

'Sort of,' I said. 'Half my class from school has just turned up.'

'So, do you know when you're on?' said Paperboy.

'Yes, second last,' I said. 'I'm not sure if that's good or not. I mean, I wouldn't want to be on first, but it's going to be a long wait.'

'You really don't want to be on first,' said a stranger's voice. The lead singer of the last band who'd sound-checked, Flash Harry, was standing next to Paperboy looking a bit sick. 'Hi, I'm Johnny,' he said.

'Hi,' I said. 'Um, you were very good in the sound-check.'

'I dunno,' said Johnny. 'I'm starting to think the rap bit isn't a good idea.'

I could have told him that, but I didn't.

'You'll be fine,' said Paperboy.

Then the stage was illuminated in a flash of pink light and Veronica walked into the middle of it.

'It's starting!' I said. 'I'd better go back ...'

'Good luck,' said Paperboy with a smile.

'Yeah,' said Johnny, looking very unwell. 'Good luck.'

'Same to you!' I said, and ran off. I reached my gang just as Veronica took the mike.

'Hi, everyone, I'm Veronica Flaherty, and welcome to this year's Knitting Factory Battle of the Bands!' said Veronica. The audience whooped and cheered. 'We've got some very talented bands for you this afternoon from all over Dublin.'

Someone in the crowd shouted, 'And Wicklow!' Then another shouted 'And Meath!'

Veronica laughed. 'Sorry, we've got people from all over the country. The winner will receive a weekend's worth of studio time in the Knitting Factory studio, complete with a sound engineer who will help you record and mix some tracks. The runner-up will get Tower Records vouchers. So there's a lot to play for! And without further ado, I'd like to welcome the first band to the stage. Please give a warm welcome to ... Flash Harry!' The crowd roared.

'That's Paperboy's friend!' I whispered to Alice, as Johnny and his bandmates made their way onto the stage. Johnny still didn't look very happy as the band started to play. They weren't bad, though. Johnny seemed to cheer up as the song went on, and his rapping bit didn't sound too terrible. I had the feeling they were going to drop the hip-hop element from their music in the future, though. We cheered loudly when they finished. As they left the stage and the next band started taking their stuff up to it, our classmates crowded around us. I couldn't believe so many had shown up. In fact, I was surprised Mrs Harrington wasn't there. For a horrible moment I wondered if she actually was, but she wasn't. Karen and Alison were, though, which was bad enough.

'So Rebecca,' said Karen in her usual smarmy voice. 'I can't wait to see your little girl band. At least I know what to expect from reading the book.'

Luckily the next band came on then, so I had an excuse not to reply to her. Which was good, because I was too wired to think of anything witty to say. We stood in silence and watched the next band for a bit. They weren't bad, but not hugely exciting. When they finished, I was turning to talk to Ellie when someone nudged me hard in the ribs. It was Cass.

'Look!' she whispered. 'It's Bike Boy's band!'

Alice was staring at them intently as they took to the stage and arranged their gear. Then Bike Boy grabbed the mike.

'Hello,' he said, in the ridiculous deep voice he'd been singing in earlier. 'I'm Richard Murray, and we're the Wicked Ways.' And they were off. I understood why Alice had found it hard to say whether they were good or not earlier. The music was good, but Bike Boy's theatrics were completely ridiculous. He was rolling his eyes and making faces as he boomed out the gloomy lyrics. It should have been hilarious. And yet ...

'I dunno,' whispered Cass. 'It kind of works.'

I knew what she meant.

'I think Bike Boy has star quality,' I whispered to Alice.

'So do I,' she whispered back. 'But ...'

Bike Boy boomed out the last note of the song and the crowd clapped and cheered.

'The audience likes him, anyway,' I said.

Behind me, I heard Karen Rodgers snort. 'The state of him!' she sniggered. 'He's like something out of a pantomime.'

Alice gave her what was, for Alice, a very dirty look. She has clearly become very proprietorial of Bike Boy already. When he finished the next song (he ended it by falling to his knees and belting out some noisy bass notes) she clapped very enthusiastically.

'Wow, quite a few bands have gone on already,' said Cass. 'I'd say we're about a third of the way through.'

I should have felt even more nervous when she said that. But it was weird. As the event went on, I started feeling more and more excited. Paperboy was mostly with Johnny, but every so often I would look over and a few times I caught him glancing in my direction. It was the first time I'd ever been in the same place as him for more than a few minutes, and I was conscious of him the entire time. I was always aware that he was in the room somewhere.

And I was also aware that I was actually looking forward to getting on stage. I mean, I was nervous, but I was genuinely excited about it. Every time another band played, we got closer to our performance time. And I found myself counting the bands, not in a 'oh no, there are only five left' way but in a 'right, only five more and then we're up' way. When I watched the bands, I realised I wanted to be up there too.

We clapped and cheered very loudly when Bad Monkey took to the stage. You couldn't tell that they were a band who, just last year, had been throwing up with nerves. They looked confident without being cocky. And they were really, really good.

'Liz is so cool,' said Cass, gazing at the stage in awe.

'She really is,' I said. When they finished, they got one of the biggest cheers of the afternoon. They stood on the stage, grinning goofily at each other for a second, before getting their stuff off the stage. The next band took their place and started to play. The lead singer was very theatrical and waily. Unlike Bike Boy, he couldn't get away with it.

'I'm going over to congratulate Bad Monkey,' said Cass. And off she went.

'You know,' I said, 'I really think this band is making us more confident. I mean, I don't think any of us would have been able to talk to strangers like that a few weeks ago.'

'I think you're right,' said Alice. She bit her lip. 'Do you think I should talk to Bike Boy?'

I looked around the room until I saw Bike Boy. He was surrounded by his band. They were having some sort of serious discussion and all looked a bit intense.

'Yes,' I said. 'But maybe wait until he's on his own.'

We stood and watched the bands for a while. I looked over at Cass, who was deep in conversation with Liz from Bad Monkey.

'There're only two bands and then it's us,' said Alice. 'We'd better get Cass.'

But Cass had obviously thought the same thing, because she was making her way back to us. When she reached us she was with Rachel and Jenny.

'Hello there,' said Rachel. 'I see we haven't managed to miss you.'

'No, worse luck,' I said. 'We're on in, like, ten minutes.'

'Oh God,' said Alice. 'I need to go to the loo.'

'Well, do it quickly,' said Cass. Alice ran off.

'Are you nervous?' asked Rachel.

'No,' I said. 'Well, a bit. But not as much as I thought I would be.'

Cass nudged me again. She nudged me so much over the course of the afternoon I bet I'll have a bruise on my side tomorrow.

'Look!' she said. I looked. And gasped, because Alice was talking to Bike Boy.

'Did she go over to him?' I said.

'No!' said Cass. 'He just came over to her!'

'We'd better stop staring in case they notice,' I said. So we looked very hard at the stage until Alice came back. She was blushing again. Cass and I looked at her meaningfully.

'Sooooo?' said Cass.

'Um, nothing,' said Alice, getting even redder. 'He just stopped me to wish me good luck.'

Cass and I looked at each other.

'Hmm,' said Cass. 'That was nice of him. Did you compliment his suit?'

Alice looked even more embarrassed. 'I did, actually. I couldn't think of anything to say. It turns out it belongs to his big brother. He's a designer or something.' The band on stage finished their second song.

'There's just one more and then us!' said Cass, as everyone clapped. 'We'd better get our stuff over to near the stage.'

'Are you on now?' whispered Ellie as we picked up our bags.

'After these guys,' said Cass. A six-piece band, complete with a girl playing the clarinet, took to the stage. 'They're going to be pretty loud so maybe everyone will be deaf by the time we go on.'

'We can but hope,' said Rachel. 'Break a leg!'

Everyone patted our shoulders or said, 'Good luck!' as we headed off towards the steps. Quite a few of them followed us to get closer to the front. The noisy band seemed to go on forever, and then it was over. And we were on next.

'And the next band is a three piece from Drumcondra in Dublin.' Vanessa's voice boomed from the speakers. 'Please welcome ... Hey Dollface!'

Our classmates cheered and jumped up and down as we climbed onto the stage. Going up the steps felt like climbing Mount Everest, and I almost tripped over some leads as

I clambered back to the drum platform and settled myself on the little stool. The lights were really, really hot and quite dazzling. I could barely see the people in the audience, which was probably a good thing. Alice and Cass got into position and turned round to me.

'Okay,' said Cass. 'This is it.' We looked at each other with wide eyes.

'Hello,' said Alice in a wobbly voice into the microphone. 'We're Hey Dollface, and this song is called "The Real Me".' There was a long pause.

'One, two, three, four!' I cried, hitting my sticks together to mark the beat, and then bashed down on the drums. Cass hit her squelchy bass line, Alice joined in with a choppy guitar, and then we all began to sing.

'They think they know me,
The real me
Just how wrong can
People be?'

From then on it all came together. There are times you play a song and it doesn't feel quite right – the energy or the excitement or the tone or something just isn't there.

But there are times when it works, and this was one of them. We were all really, really into what we were doing. I was playing the drums with all my might, and even though it was too hot under the lights and drumming so hard made me hotter, I didn't care. It felt brilliant. It felt as though we were acting out the music. There's a bit towards the end of the song where it sort of pauses, but I keep drumming and then Cass's bass line kicks in and then Alice's guitar, and at that moment we all turned to look at each other and we were just beaming, like we couldn't believe how much fun this was. It was, I am not exaggerating, one of the best moments of my life. When I looked out in the crowd I saw Ellie and Emma and Jessie at the very front and realised that they were – could they be? – yes! They were doing a synchronised dance! It turns out that if there's anything cooler than taking part in a synchronised public dance routine, it's playing the music that people are doing one to. Rachel and Jenny were standing nearby, tapping their feet to the beat. And I could also see, out of the corner of my eye, Paperboy. He was standing with Johnny to one side of the stage, and he was smiling too, in a really nice, pleased way. I usually avoid the cymbals as much as possible because they're really hard to play, but when we reached the end of the song I stretched out and bashed one as hard as I could. We'd done it. We'd played our first live song. And we ROCKED.

As soon as we finished, the crowd started cheering and whooping. Ellie and Emma and Jessie were leaping up and down and Paperboy was clapping like mad. Even Rachel was waving her fist in the air and hollering. I'd never seen anything like it. I couldn't see Karen anywhere, but I'd like to think she was feeling sick. Although if she was, she was going to cheer up quite a lot in a few minutes, as you will see.

'Um, thanks very much,' said Cass. 'Our next song is a cover. And it's an old song. But it's a very good one.'

I hit the sticks to count us in and we started to play. Alice was just battering her guitar and sounded absolutely great. I was thumping away, but after a few seconds I became aware that the little stool I was sitting on was wobbling a bit. It had also moved a bit further back from the drum kit. I ignored it and kept drumming, but I got a bit distracted and made a little mistake. Cass glanced over at me for a second, and that was when the stool wobbled a little bit more, and one of its legs reached the edge of the drum platform. And before I knew it, it had fallen over the edge. And so had I. I tumbled backwards straight off the little platform and landed in an uncomfortable heap.

I shrieked, the drumsticks went flying, the crowd roared in horror (or possibly laughter), and Cass and Alice stopped playing immediately. Cass ran over while Alice tried to get her guitar strap over her head.

'Bex!' she cried, peering over the drums. 'Bex, are you alive?'

From the crowd I could hear gasps and shocked voices and the odd giggle. Then silence.

I rubbed my head and sat up. I couldn't believe it. I'd just fallen over in front of hundreds of people. Including Paperboy. I thought I had already been as embarrassed as it was physically possible to be, but now I found out I had been wrong. This was worse than anything to do with Mum's book. I sat there in a daze. I didn't want to move. I wanted to hide behind the drums forever.

'Rebecca, are you okay?' said Paul the sound guy, who had run onto the stage. 'Do you need a doctor?'

'I'm fine,' I said, standing up, just to make sure I could. 'Ow! No, I'm fine, really. I didn't hit my head. I'm okay.' I was, miraculously. Well, I felt awful, obviously, but it was more embarrassment than anything else.

'Come on, Bex, we'll get you a glass of water or something,' said Alice.

'No,' I said. 'Come on, we've got to keep going.'

'After that?' said Cass.

'I'll feel worse if we stop,' I said.

'Guys?' said Paul. 'Do you want to go on?'

'Yes,' said Alice. 'Come on.' She grabbed the mike as I sat back behind the drum kit (on a spare chair Paul had grabbed from the side of the stage – he'd taken away the stupid wobbly stool) and Cass handed me the drumsticks, which had landed on her keyboard.

'So, as we were saying,' said Alice, and I counted us in and started playing again and everyone in the audience cheered.

If we were in a film, this would have been the bit where we played better than we'd ever played before. But we weren't, and we didn't. In fact, we were pretty crap. I still felt all shaky and I couldn't get that brilliant feeling from earlier, the feeling that you're three people all making the same sound. It all sounded detached and just ... off. Our harmonies went a bit wobbly and we all made a few mistakes on our instruments and botched notes. I think we were all just wishing for it to be over. When it was, the audience gave us a huge cheer, but I still felt awful. The embarrassment of falling and then playing really badly almost cancelled out the fun of the first song.

'I'm so, so sorry,' I kept saying, as we made our way to a quiet bit of the hall near the loos and the last band, The Retreat, started to play. I was almost in tears.

'It wasn't your fault,' said Alice. 'It was that wobbly stool.'

'No one else fell off,' I pointed out.

'Well, it was only a matter of time before someone did,' said Cass. 'It was just bad luck that it was you.'

'Ooh,' said Alice. 'Paperboy is on his way over.'

'Oh God,' I said. 'Is there any way I can avoid him? Can I run to the loo?'

'Not really,' said Alice. 'He's sort of between us and the toilets.' I looked up and saw Paperboy heading our way, raising his hand in greeting. But just before he reached us, a ferocious figure barged through the crowd, accompanied by two miserable-looking adults and one slightly embarrassed-looking minion.

It was Vanessa. 'I don't believe it!' she screamed. 'You've just made a complete fool of me!'

'I've made ... what?' I said, completely bewildered.

'You fell over!' roared Vanessa.

'Um, I know,' I said. 'I was there.' I could see Paperboy standing behind them, looking very confused.

'I've been telling these guys how professional and talented you are!' Vanessa went on. 'And then you go and humiliate me like that in front of them! You can't even sit on a chair without falling over! I'm ... I'm so disappointed in you, Becca.'

'What?' I said.

'You're meant to be my friend, and you're meant to be playing at my party,' said Vanessa, actually stamping her stiletto-shod foot. 'And now you've ruined everything!' She was jumping up and down now. I'd never seen anything like it.

'Vanessa, I ...' I began. But Vanessa wasn't finished. 'You were meant to be my ... my Unique Selling Point because your mother wrote that book about you! But you haven't sold anything! Except falling over like an idiot!

You've ruined my chance to be famous, Becca!'

That was it.

'My name,' I roared, 'is not Becca!'

Vanessa stared at me. So did her entourage.

'I told you last week that I wasn't going to play at your crazy party,' I shouted. 'We're not friends, and you never even spoke to me until you decided my mother had written a book about me. Well, I've got news for you, Vanessa. That book is not about me. I'm not Ruthie O'Reilly, I'm not famous, I'm just me! Rebecca, by the way, not Becca! And I just fell over in front of four hundred people! So pardon me for not caring about you and your stupid TV programme and your pink pony and your stupid crane!'

And I ran away into the girls' bathroom. On the way, I passed Paperboy, who was staring at me in shock. Brilliant, I thought. Now he thinks I'm as crazy as Vanessa. As well as someone who's just humiliated herself in front of almost everyone she knows. I ran into a cubicle and locked the door. I'll just stay in here until it's over, I thought. And I felt so sorry for myself that tears started to trickle down my face. Then I remembered what Rachel had said about the eye make-up. Brilliant. That's all I needed, to cover myself in black mascara streaks. I snuffled and tried to dab my eyes with a bit of loo roll.

Then I heard Rachel, Cass and Alice calling me through the door.

'Come on out, Bex,' said Alice. 'No one cares about Vanessa!'

'What about the fact that I just fell over and showed my pants in front of four hundred people?' I sniffled.

'You didn't, you were wearing tights,' said Cass. 'And they don't care about that either.'

'Seriously, Bex, they don't,' said Rachel. 'It's fine. To be honest, I think people are kind of impressed.'

'What?' I said. 'They don't think I did it on purpose as a stunt, do they?'

'Well, no,' said Rachel. 'But they're impressed that you didn't, like, cry and run away.'

'I don't care,' I said. 'I'm not coming out of here until everyone's gone home.'

'Oh, come on, Bex,' said Alice. 'They're going to announce the winner in a minute!'

'Maybe they'll give us an award for most embarrassing performance,' I said, sniffing.

I heard the door of the bathroom open and then Ellie's voice. 'I think we're going to find out who won now,' she said.

'Bex?' said Cass.

'I'm staying here,' I said. I couldn't go out now. I was probably covered in streaks, for one.

'Look, we've got to go and see,' said Cass. 'Follow us out, okay?'

'Do you want me to stay here?' said Rachel. She is not a bad sister, really.

'No, it's okay,' I said. I didn't say anything for a moment, but she was still there. 'Thanks.'

''Sokay,' said Rachel. 'Seriously, you should come out.'

'I can't,' I said. I could hear cheering coming from the hall. 'I think I cried my eyeliner all over my face.'

Rachel sighed. 'Come on, let me see.'

I opened the door of the cubicle.

'Oh,' said Rachel. 'Apparently that crap is more waterproof than I thought. It's only smudged a little bit under your eye. Hang on a sec.' And she rummaged in her ginormous bag and pulled out a pack of cleansing wipes.

'Come here,' she said, and carefully ran the wipe under

my eyes. 'There. You're grand.'

'I'm not really,' I said. 'Rache, I know you and the others think it's not a big deal, but it's not just the falling over. Paperboy saw Vanessa screeching at me. And he must have seen me screeching back at her. He must think I'm mad, as well as an idiot who can't even sit on a stool without falling off it.'

'No, he won't think that,' said Rachel. She was doing her wise big sister voice, but for once I didn't mind too much.

'It's not just that either,' I said. 'I really wanted to show everyone at school that I could do something cool and different that had nothing to do with Ruthie O'Reilly and Mum's stupid book. And I couldn't even do that properly. Everyone in school is going to think this is hilarious.'

'Well, at least you've given them something else to talk about,' said Rachel.

'Shut up,' I said. I sighed. 'Do you think everyone's gone yet?'

'Um, no,' said Rachel. 'We've only been here for about two seconds. From all the cheering I think they're still announcing the winner. Don't you want to see who won?'

'I suppose so,' I said. And we went out. The Retreat were strutting around the stage.

'Huh,' I said. 'They must have won.'

There was no sign of Paperboy anywhere. But Cass and Alice were just outside.

'We didn't win,' said Cass. 'Obviously, as those silly boys are on the stage now looking like they've just won the World Cup. But Bad Monkey and Bike Boy's band came joint second! Apparently the judges couldn't decide between them.'

'Oh,' I said. 'Well, that's pretty cool, I suppose.' I looked at my watch. 'Wow, my mum will be out there to collect us in a few minutes. We should get our stuff together and go home.'

'I wish we hadn't arranged for her to get us so early,' said Alice. 'I wouldn't mind going for a coffee or something.'

'With who?' said Cass. 'Us or your special new friend, Bike Boy?'

'His name's Richard, actually,' said Alice. And that was when I saw what seemed like our entire class heading in our direction.

'Oh no,' I muttered. 'Quick, let's go.' But it was too late. We were surrounded.

'Oh my God,' said Jessie Mc Cabe. 'You were amazing!'

'What?' I said.

'Seriously, you were so good!' said Catherine Wallace. 'I can't believe you actually got up after you fell over. Are you okay, by the way?'

'Um, yeah, I'm fine,' I said. 'But ...'

'You were so brilliant!' said Ellie. 'Really! Didn't you see our dance?'

'Yes,' I said. 'It was fantastic. But ...'

I tried to explain how terrible we'd been in the second song, but no one seemed to care. Everyone was hugging us and telling us how much they were looking forward to our next gig. Liz from Bad Monkey came over to say well done. Maybe, I thought, things weren't so bad after all. I mean, Paperboy was probably going to avoid me for the rest of my life, but at least it looked like people in school had forgotten about Mum's book for a while. Well, some of them.

'Well done, Rebecca,' said Karen Rodgers. 'I'm pretty sure your lookalike Ruthie wouldn't have fallen over like that. You really are an original.'

'Oh my God, Karen, SHUT UP,' said an unfamiliar voice. We all looked around in surprise until we realised it had come from Alison, Karen's sidekick. The reason it sounded so unfamiliar was because we'd never heard her talk like that before. She didn't sound like a sidekick at all. We all stared at her, including Karen. 'Just leave her alone,' said Alison, sounding a bit more timid, as though she couldn't believe what she'd just said.

Karen blinked. 'Oh,' she said. 'Um, okay then.' She looked a bit embarrassed. But I didn't have time to wonder what this meant for the future because Cass was in front of me beaming.

'Listen to this,' she said. 'I was just talking to Liz again, and she suggested that we do a gig with Bad Monkey soon. Like, a full gig, just the two of us.'

'Wow,' I said. Could we do a full gig? I suppose it wouldn't be too scary if the drums were flat on the ground and not on a stupid platform.

'We'll have to write a lot more songs,' said Alice.

'Well, if we need inspiration, you can ask your new friend Richard,' said Cass with a snigger.

'Shuddup,' said Alice, going bright red.

My phone beeped. I checked my texts. 'It's Mum,' I said. 'She's going to be outside, around the corner from the main entrance, in about five minutes.'

'Right,' said Cass. 'Well, I've got Liz's e-mail address, so I said we'd be in touch with her soon. But that's cool about doing a gig, right?'

'Yeah,' I said. I thought about it for a second. And I forgot about the awfulness of falling over and playing badly. I remembered the bit in the first song where it all worked perfectly. I thought about doing that again. 'Wow, yeah, it really is.'

We said goodbye to our classmates (not including Karen, who was looking a bit sheepish) and gathered our stuff together. Rachel and Jenny were going off somewhere fancy and grown up (well, it was somewhere that lets in sixteen-year-olds, so I suppose it can't be too fancy), so they weren't getting a lift. I looked around for Paperboy on the way out, but there was no sign of him. He'd probably gone home in horror, after seeing Vanessa roaring at me like I was the worst person in the world. We waved at Bad Monkey and they waved back.

'Don't forget to mail me!' cried Liz.

‘I won’t!’ said Cass. She beamed at me and Alice. ‘We’ve already started our own music scene.’

‘I wouldn’t go that far,’ said Alice. ‘But another gig would be very cool.’

When we reached the entrance hall we met Robbie, the ‘My Big Birthday Bash’ bloke.

‘Oh, hello,’ he said. ‘Are you okay?’

‘I’m fine,’ I said. ‘Um, sorry about that earlier.’

‘Oh, don’t worry about it,’ he said.

‘How is Vanessa?’ said Alice.

A look of pain passed over Robbie’s face. ‘She’s fine. She’s more than fine, actually. We told her we’re definitely going to feature her in the show.’

We were all so startled Cass and I nearly dropped her keyboard.

‘You’re what?’ I said.

‘She’s, well, she’s highly strung, but she’ll be television gold,’ said Robbie. He looked at us hopefully. ‘I don’t suppose there’s any way you’d go and play at her party?’

‘No,’ I said.

‘Really? Oh well, she’s enough on her own. She’s hiring a tank, you know.’

'Yes, I heard,' I said.

'And that pony too ... It should be impressive. Anyway, I'll let you get on. Nice meeting you!' And off he went.

'Words fail me,' said Cass.

'Me too,' I said. 'She's going to be worse than ever now.'

Mum was already parked around the corner when we got there.

'So,' she said. 'How did it go?'

'Meh,' I said.

'We were great,' said Cass.

'Apart from when I fell backwards and nearly wrecked the entire thing,' I said, opening the boot so we could put Cass's keyboard in it.

'What?' said Mum. 'Are you okay?'

'Yeah, yeah, I'm fine,' I said. 'It was just embarrassing.'

Mum asked lots of predictable Mum questions about whether I could be concussed or have any broken bones, and by the time she was satisfied that I wasn't going to drop dead or lose a limb, we had got our stuff into the car. I was just about to get into the car myself when I realised I'd forgotten my jacket.

'I left it hanging off that amp at the side of the stage,' I said. 'I hope it's still there. That's all I need, losing my favourite jacket.'

'Oh dear,' said Mum. 'Okay, well, hurry up and run back and get it. I'll wait here.'

So I ran back around the corner and into the venue. There were still a good few people hanging around, but I couldn't see Paperboy anywhere. I could see my jacket, though, safe and sound on the amp. I got it and headed back out, wondering if I would ever talk to Paperboy again, or whether he had been put off me forever by (a) the fact that Vanessa Finn had turned up with TV producers and pretended we were best mates (b) I had made a holy show of myself on stage or (c) all of the above. If he had, which seemed very likely, I'd just have to stop answering the door on Fridays. It wouldn't be that hard. I could just try and forget about him.

And then, just as I was coming out of the venue and feeling very sorry for myself, I met Paperboy coming in. It was like that time at Tower Records, except this time he wasn't with an intimidating ex-girlfriend. He was on his own.

'Oh, hi!' he said. 'I was looking for you.'

As usual, I couldn't think of anything intelligent to say to this, so I just said, 'Oh, really?'

'Yes,' he said. 'I wanted to tell you that you and the band were brilliant.'

'What, even when I fell over in front of everyone I know?'

'Especially then,' said Paperboy with a grin. 'It was a very impressive fall. Like a stuntwoman. Also, you might remember that you got up and kept playing.'

'Well, it was either that or burst into tears,' I said. 'And if I'd done that, crazy Vanessa would probably have killed me. She'd have run me over in her pink tank.'

'Yeah, what was wrong with that girl?' said Paperboy. 'She's a bit scary. She's not really friends with you, is she? I mean, she seems a bit ... intense.'

'No,' I said. 'She wanted to pretend we were friends so the TV producers would put her in their programme. It's a long story. And now they're going to put her in anyway!'

'Wow, really?' said Paperboy. 'You're not going to be in it too, are you?'

'God, no!' I said in horror, and Paperboy laughed.

'Well, if you were, at least it'd be entertaining,' he said.

And then he looked a bit serious. I realised we were standing very close together.

'Rebecca ...' he said. 'Um. There's something I've wanted to do for ages.'

And then, in broad daylight, outside the Knitting Factory in the middle of town, he kissed me.

HE KISSED ME!

I have been kissed by Paperboy! And it was lovely, although I wasn't sure exactly what I was doing. After all, I've never kissed anyone before. I don't think I was very good. But I didn't get a chance to improve because while he was kissing me and I was trying to kiss him back, I heard our car horn beeping and heard the awful voice of my mother going, 'Bex! Come on!'

The car was just a few feet away with the window rolled down. She was meant to be around the corner! What was she doing here? I jumped away from Paperboy as if I'd been electrocuted.

'I'm coming!' I cried in a croaky voice. I looked back at Paperboy. 'I, um, I'd better go,' I said.

'Okay,' said Paperboy. He looked a bit embarrassed too. But also quite happy. 'I'd better get back in to Johnny and the others. They're still inside. So ... will I see you soon? And not just in a, well, paper-money-collecting capacity?'

'Oh!' I said. I am very bad at all this. Maybe I should have asked Rachel for advice in the ways of love before now. But I didn't seriously think I'd ever get to use it. 'Yes please.'

'Rebecca!' said my mother. 'I'm parking illegally here!' I could see Cass and Alice in the back seat tapping her on the shoulder and whispering urgently in her ear.

'I'm coming!' I said. 'So ... will I see you on Friday?'

'Definitely,' said Paperboy. 'And maybe we can arrange to meet somewhere less, um, full of your angry relatives.'

'Okay,' I said. He grinned at me and kissed me on the cheek.

'See you then,' he said, and headed back into the venue. He had just reached the door when I remembered something.

'Hey!' I called out. 'I know this is ridiculous but ... what's your name?'

He laughed and turned back for a second.

'It's ...' And just as he spoke my horrible, awful

embarrassing mother blasted the car horn. By the time she'd stopped blasting he was inside the building and I had to get in the car, where Cass and Alice shrieked so loudly my mother threatened to kick us all out. Which is just like her. I can't believe she's done it again! Just when I thought she had stopped disgracing me in public.

I also can't believe I have been kissed by Paperboy and I still don't know what his name is.

Oh well.

I'll find out on Friday.

THE END